I0717210

REPLAY

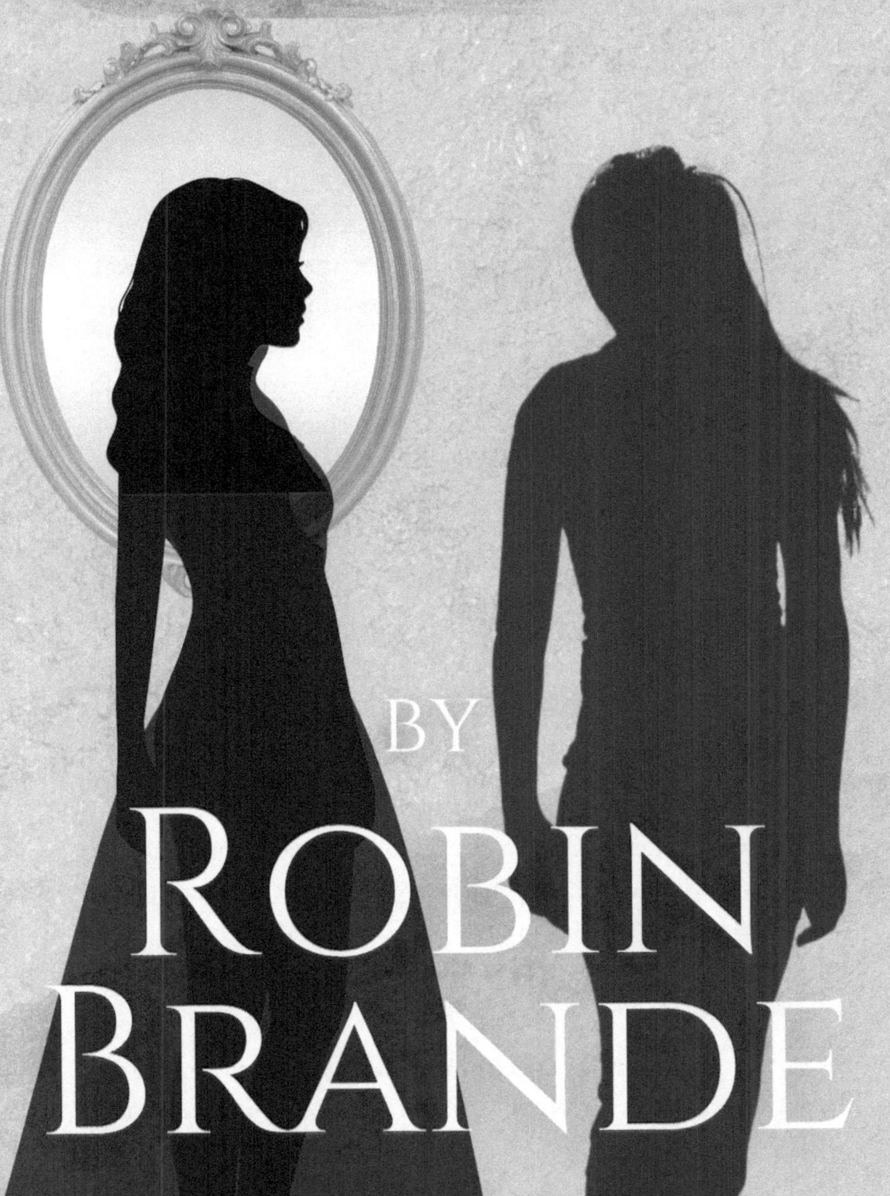

BY

ROBIN BRANDE

REPLAY
By Robin Brande

Published by Ryer Publishing
www.ryerpublishing.com
Anniversary Edition © 2026 by Robin Brande
robinbrande.com
All rights reserved.
Cover art by Jacob Gregory/Dreamstime
Danyl Sasmita, Iconic Prototype, Fajarari, formatoriginalphotos, OpenClipart-Vectors, KatarzynaTyl, Hikmat Studios, ragamara, RM Creative, iconpix, Iryna Shancheva, tsapenko1129, Xenia, oksanavectorart, buings, Tatyana Yagudina, Jasmine023, Vector Tradition, Icons8, GDJ, med.asf, Rizkreativ, and Marie Dautel/Canva
Cover design by Ryer Publishing
ISBN: 978-1-952383-20-5

ALSO BY ROBIN BRANDE

YOUNG ADULT STANDALONES

DOGGIRL
EVOLUTION, ME &
OTHER FREAKS OF NATURE
FAT CAT

YOUNG ADULT SERIES

~PARALLELOGRAM QUARTET~
INTO THE PARALLEL
CAUGHT IN THE PARALLEL
SEIZE THE PARALLEL
BEYOND THE PARALLEL

REPLAY

1

I died. For forty-two seconds I died.

They were operating on me—why isn't important anymore—and it was a simple surgery, everyone said so. My dad didn't even take off work.

Breathing, breathing, not.

I can picture it. The "oh, no," the scurrying around, the paddles on my chest, *thwump*. Clear! *Thwump. Beep beep, beep beep,* she's back. Everything back to normal.

They don't know anything.

2

People think they understand time. They think it always means the same thing: sixty seconds in a minute, sixty minutes in an hour, the same everywhere, in every universe, in every situation because we say so.

But it's not true. I know that now. Time is a line, stretching out forever. It's fluid. It's loose. It stretches and it bends, and seconds in one place can be hours in another.

They'll say I was just hallucinating. That my brain was deprived of oxygen, and it made pretty pictures for me, and what I saw wasn't real. But I know what I know. I was there. And it was as real as anything I've ever been through in my life.

They're all so careful not to talk about it. Forty-two

seconds gone from my life, and no one even thinks to ask where I was?

Well, almost no one. For the first couple of days, Beth was all over me.

"What was it like? Could you tell you were dead? Did you see anything?"

I always lied, even though I'm not supposed to do that anymore. But I just don't think my thirteen-year-old sister can handle what really happened to me. Especially since I'm not really sure myself.

So I told her I didn't know anything was going on. That it was just like being asleep.

"Did you dream?"

"No, not really."

Beth is not known for giving up. "So you didn't feel anything? You couldn't tell that something was wrong? You didn't feel . . . different?"

No, no, and no.

But of course the answer's yes. Yes to all of it: Yes I felt it, yes I knew, yes everything has changed.

Because now I understand Time. And how meaningless it is. And that I'm such a small part of it. This one life of mine—this Cara Lily Campbell life, 616 N. Waverly Street, Pinedale, Colorado, born February 3rd, parents Ron and Gretchen, sister Beth—this life is just one tiny speck of a moment among the huge vastness of Time, and for sixteen years I've been acting like my stupid life is the biggest deal in the world.

Well, I'm over that.

It's hard to hang on to your delusions when you die on the operating table and find yourself a naked blob of light plopped down in the middle of a card game with four other naked blobs of light in a cold gray place that might be heaven, although I'm still not sure. That's one of the things I have to figure out.

That, and why I woke up thinking about David.

The game was already going when I arrived. I dropped in like I'd been there all along. No one even looked up. They just accepted that I wasn't there a second ago and now I was, deal me in, carry on. No, "Oh, hi, Cara, you're dead, nice to see you." Just flip me a card and expect me to know what to do with it.

It melted. A regular playing card—ten of clubs—and it melted right into me like the card was made of my own skin. Which, it turns out, it was.

All the cards in that round were made of skin. The jack of diamonds—brown. Three of hearts—black. Eight of spades—white. Nine of clubs—tan. The four people playing with me all drew cards and all got skin to go with the bodies they were about to win in the next round, but mine wouldn't take. My card melted right away and left me what I was, just a glowing mass of light, no body to me at all, no face, no hair, no nothing.

"Because you're not dead," one of them told me—the pale one who had drawn the eight of spades. "Your body's still down there—you're not done with it yet." She drew another card and grew a torso and legs and breasts and all the rest, and long brown hair and brown eyes.

It was gray where we were—overcast and colorless, no wind, no warmth, just gray. No light except what was coming from us—even after they had their bodies on, I could still see light seeping through. We sat around a table made of mottled gray marble that was too cold to the touch. I shivered every time I reached for a card.

New deal. The man on my left read out his—two of hearts. "Musician," they all agreed as a patch of blue appeared where his heart should have been.

The next one drew Mathematician. Next one, Healer. And the woman picked Teacher, which seemed to make her happy.

I drew three cards in a row, but none of them mattered. They all melted away.

"You already drew before," the woman explained. "You're already set."

Another round of play. This one was for place of birth. Darfur, New Delhi, Washington, D.C. The minute they read out their cards, the three men were gone, leaving just her and me.

"Aren't you going to draw?" I asked.

"No, I think I'll stay with you," she said. "Until it's time for you go back."

Meanwhile, someone in the operating room had just figured it out. I heard him off in the distance. "We lost the heartbeat!"

Good, I thought. This might take a while.

4

I don't know about anyone else who's died and come back to life, but all I want is cheese.

Smooth, tangy, creamy, soft, orange or white—it's all I've been eating for the past week, despite my mother's badgering. When I first got home from the hospital I sat down and ate half a package of longhorn cheddar. Oh my God, heaven.

Cheese and sleep. I must have slept eighteen hours yesterday. Mom says I don't have to go back to school until I feel a hundred percent strong. They're used to me gutting it out, all those injuries over the years—the torn ACL, the broken wrist, the sprains and dislocations, everything else—so if I'm sleeping this much, they must figure I need it. The doctor told them that after a trauma—even a short one like mine—the body can need a long time to recover. Fine. I'll take it. I have other things to do.

Like this morning. I sat out on the porch with my leg propped up, drinking tea, staring at the aspens in front of our house and really trying to understand them. That pale cool bark. The perfect construction of the leaves with their spindly stems that let them twist and flutter in the wind like fans whipping back and forth. Who decided on aspens? There are enough trees in the world, so why those? Is it just because they're beautiful? God or someone decided hey, I need something white and green here, with some shimmer to it, and so bam, we have the aspen, ladies and gentlemen, hope you enjoy it.

Same with the birds. So many unnecessary varieties of them. The colors, the beaks, the wing patterns, the calls and cries, the bug-eaters and the nut-crackers and all the rest. Why? Isn't the world busy enough? Why do we need wrens *and* parrots *and* ostriches? It's obscene, it's so overdone.

So I sat there looking at the pines and the aspens and listening to all the competing species of birds, and meanwhile somewhere in a high school three miles from here hundreds of teenagers were walking around in their own particular varieties—with and without zits, with blue eyes and brown eyes, boobs and no boobs, brains and no brains, everyone so worried about how they look and how everyone else sees them, and WHAT'S THE POINT?

And here I was, boobs of my own, green eyes, blond hair, and who cares? Because they're all disposable. They don't mean anything. They're all just a flip of the cards.

I can't tell anyone these thoughts. There are too many of them and most are clearly crazy—"Why are there birds? Why does anyone love me? Did I ever matter in this world?"—and meanwhile I smile and say thank you for the grilled cheese (which I keep scraping off the bread—not ready for bread yet), and try to keep it together until I can go to sleep again.

And then on top of all that, I can't stop thinking about David.

And tell me that's not crazy. We're talking David Mayer here—bad clothes, bad hair, the guy who always smells like garlic and paint. That specimen.

So why was his face the one that flashed across my brain just as I was coming back to life? Not my parents, not my sister, not my friends, but David flippin' Mayer. A guy I've never spoken more than three words to in my life.

But it has to mean something, right? You don't just see a face for no reason as you're flying back into your body.

So what am I supposed to do about it? Call him up, say, "Hey, David, want to hear something funny?" And then what comes after that? Does he have some message for me? Some series of tasks I'm supposed to complete, like Hercules? *"Bring me the head of Gargantua . . ."*

Reincarnation for Amateurs—that's what I need. Some sort of manual to tell me how I'm supposed to be and act and think anymore. It can't be that when you survive your own death all you're meant to do with your life is sleep, eat cheese, and stare at trees all day.

Maybe I should call David.

At some point.

5

____

"Hey," Beth said, plopping her backpack onto the porch and sinking into the wicker chair beside mine. She was careful not to come anywhere near my leg, outstretched on the padded wicker footstool.

"How was school?" I asked.

"The usual. Seriously," she said, pointing to the plate of cheese on my lap, "is that all you're ever going to eat anymore?"

"Maybe."

"Maybe not."

She reached into her backpack and brought out an assortment of chocolate bars, fanned out in her hands like playing cards.

"From that bakery by Dad's," she said.

"I could totally marry you right now."

We didn't gorge. Beth and I set up a proper chocolate sampling station on little table between our chairs, and we took our time working from one end of the selections to the other. The hazelnut/raisin combo. White and dark chocolate swirls. Milk chocolate over cookie with a caramel center, and plain milk chocolate that was anything but plain as it melted on my tongue and went directly into my blood stream and knitted together some of the gaps I've been feeling between nerve endings that have been making me so jittery lately.

By the end of the third bar I felt warm again. Almost happy. I didn't realize how cold I've been these last few days—really, ever since I came back. It's like my blood still hasn't even returned to room temperature yet.

"I have a theory," I told Beth, because I'd just come up with it and felt like telling someone besides myself. I've been alone inside my head for too long. It felt good to talk again.

"Let's hear it," she said with her mouth full.

"I think when you die and you come back—"

Beth's eyes widened ever so slightly. I'd introduced the D word.

"—I think after that you're assigned one section of the alphabet, and you have to eat off of it the rest of your life. I obviously got the 'ch's. Cheese, chocolate—"

"Oh, right," she said, "so, Chex Mix, Cheerios—"

"Chick peas—"

"Chives—"

"Chestnuts," I said.

"Chicken—"

That stopped me. "No. No chicken. Ever. No meat of any kind. That sounds repulsive." Until I said it, I didn't realize that's how I felt. Considering that I've always eaten anything and everything—in massive quantities sometimes, depending on how long and hard I've pushed it all day—it was as much of a surprise to me as to Beth.

"Why?"

"I don't know," I said. "Just the thought of eating flesh right now makes me want to gag."

"Maybe you're more . . . sensitive," Beth ventured, looking at me out of the corner of her eye. I could see she wasn't sure how far she could go. My parents must have said something to her before about all her questions. "You know, since . . ."

I ripped open the chocolate macadamia nut. "All right, Bethie, ask."

"Ask what?" she said all innocently.

"I know you've been waiting. So go ahead."

"Really?"

I nodded, and she launched right into it.

"Okay, so do you still feel weird? I mean, you've been all spaced out ever since you came back. Half the time I don't know if you're in a trance or sleeping or what. I mean, we talk to you and it's like you can't hear us or you don't care or whatever. And then sometimes I can see you're talking to yourself, but your lips don't really move, it's just your eyebrows crinkle up, or you shake your head or frown or act like you're having this really intense conversation with someone. Can you see people now? Like, dead people? Are they talking to you?"

I snorted. "No."

"Because it's okay if you are," she assured me. "I won't tell Mom and Dad. But I just wonder what's going on, you know? I mean, you died. You were really dead—no joke. You could have stayed dead. Is it one of those things where you have to actually decide if you want to come back?"

My head was starting to hurt. Maybe it was the chocolate rush, maybe it was so many words all at once after a full week of relative quiet. But I couldn't just blow off my little sister again. I'm sure I'd have been just as curious if she were the one who had died.

So I gave her a little something. "I don't think it was my time yet."

"Yeah, but how did you know?"

Because I met a woman or an angel or some sort of celestial being, and she told me I was only there for a little while so she could basically talk some sense into me and then slap me on the butt and send me home. And someday, Bethie, when you die, you're going to go to this strange place where you'll play cards with a bunch of blobs of light, and that's how you'll find out everything you're supposed to be in your next life. Isn't that cool? Doesn't that freak you out? Now let's have some more chocolate.

But I didn't say any of that. Because a part of me thinks maybe I'm not supposed to tell—maybe everyone is supposed to find out for themselves. And another part of me thinks it's hard enough to deal with all that when you're sixteen, and I don't really need to burden my little sister with it.

And a part of me just plain thinks it's private. Maybe I'm selfish. Maybe I want to hold it close to me as long as I can.

"Bethie, I'm getting kind of tired—"

"Oh, okay," she said, clearly disappointed. She swung her legs over the arm of her chair and started to stand up.

"Sit," I said between my teeth. A car had just pulled up.

6

"Hey, Cara Dara!" It was Toomy.

"Don't let her stay too long," I muttered to Beth, "okay? Tell her I get too tired or something."

Beth gave me a strange look, which I understood, since Toomy has been my best friend since second grade.

"Ten minutes," I said, "okay?"

I'd barely gotten it out before Toomy bounded onto the porch. She glanced at my leg and winced. "Yow, gimp." She slapped my hand in greeting. "What's shakin', Bethie?"

"Not much." Beth left us to go back inside, but not before tapping her watch at me, a little too theatrically.

"Okay, I promise." I rolled my eyes at Toomy. "Nurse Campbell says I'm not to exert myself."

Toomy noticed the plate on my lap, piled high with provolone and chocolate wrappers.

"Fully lettin' yourself go, huh?"

"Yeah," I said. "Want some?"

Toomy chuffed. "I could so kick your ass at the hundred right now."

And so it resumed. This weird combination the two of us have—part friendship, part competition. And the truth is I'm not interested in either anymore.

Toomy launched into her report about everything that's been going on at school while I've been gone, and I just didn't care. It meant as much to me as if she'd shown up to discuss Bangladeshi weather. As weird as I feel around my own family right now, I can't even imagine what it will be like when I have to go back to school. I have nothing in common with any of those people anymore. I feel about a hundred years old.

And while Toomy was babbling away I was busy thinking, *I wonder why her eyes are brown. Why her top lip is bigger than the bottom one. Which card she drew to get that pitching arm. Does she already know what she is? Did she pick Healer? Or Mother? Or maybe Killer? How many choices are in that deck? How specific does it get? Was Hitler born Hitler?*

Toomy waved her hand in front of my face. "Hey— stoner—you listening?"

"Yeah," I lied. "Just a little tired."

Right on cue, thank you, Beth emerged from the house to point at her watch again. "Sorry," she told me, "but you know what the doctor said."

"Aye, aye," I answered, saluting. "Sorry, Toom, my jailer is very strict."

Toomy didn't budge yet. "Alex been by?"

"Nope." I let out a breath. I'd been waiting for that question.

"Huh? What's up with that?"

"I'm sure he's busy." I felt like adding, *"Good."*

"I'll go ride his ass," Toomy promised.

"No, that's okay—"

"Happy to." She stood up, took another serious look at my leg, and said, "How long do they think?"

"Months. At least through skiing, maybe into softball."

Toomy whistled. "My dad's not gonna like that."

I shrugged. "I'm not having much fun with it, either."

She slapped my hand again and set off. "I'm gonna go rag on your boy. Not coming over—what a dog."

"It's okay," I called after her. "Don't bother."

But she was already dialing him on her cell. She waved over her shoulder. "No problem. He deserves some hell."

I sank back in my chair. I really was exhausted.

Beth must have noticed. "Want some help?"

"Nah, I'm okay. Just hand me those." Beth waited with my crutches while I gingerly lifted my leg from the footstool. "Hey, by the way—thanks for breaking it up."

"Are you mad at her or something?"

"No. It's just . . . I can't really take all the noise anymore. It's too much talking."

Beth must have thought that included her, too, because she didn't say anything else as she followed me inside and up the stairs. But she did suck in her breath every time it looked like I might bump my leg. Finally I had to tell her she was making me nervous.

"Sorry, it just looks so . . . painful."

"I have to get used to it," I said. "I'm going to be on these for a while."

When we were finally outside my bedroom, Beth asked, "Do you want me to call you for dinner?"

"No, I think I'm just going to sleep. I'll come down later if I'm hungry."

"You don't have to do that," she said. "Just shout. I'll bring you something."

How could you not love a sister like that? So why couldn't it have been her face I saw as I came back to life? It would have made everything so much easier.

I shut my bedroom door and leaned against it. I really did want to go back to bed, but I knew I had to do something first—something I should have done days ago. There's really no way of escaping it.

I went to my computer, did a quick search, and found David Mayer's phone number. Because obviously the card I drew was Stalker.

Great start to my new life. I'm hunting down a freak.

7

Okay, so to be fair, David isn't the worst guy at my school. That distinction would belong to Pete Allred, the guy who lives near the fish hatchery and always shows up reeking of b.o. and spawn. Major zits. A really thick nose and wide nostrils—*that* would be a problem if I'd woken up thinking about him. David isn't disgusting, he's just . . . wrong.

He showed up freshman year, an import from Denver, and I suppose we weren't exactly welcoming, but David didn't help his case any by acting like he was Big City and we were just a bunch of hillbillies who ate our own dogs in the winter. Massive GPA, which didn't add to his charm as far as a lot of people were concerned. Didn't take long to bring him down. Alex and the rest of the guys made sure of it.

Toomy played her part, too. And I suppose I did, too, although I really didn't want to bother. When someone is an insignificant little worm, isn't it easier to just step over him than on him? But whatever. A little well-timed laughter every time he spoke in class, some significant looks and sarcastic smiles between all of us every time he passed—it didn't take long for people to figure out this one Didn't Belong. And David seemed to get it, too. He pretty much faded into the background after the first few weeks. Other than when he's called on in class, I don't think I've heard the guy speak the last two years.

So it wasn't without some fear that I dialed his number.

And of course he was home, because where would a guy like him go after school? It was half past four, and he probably already had all his homework done. For the next month.

"Hi . . . David?"

"Speaking."

"Oh. Hi. It's Cara. Campbell."

Silence. Then finally, "Cara Campbell."

"From calc?"

"Yes, I know."

That was it. Silence once again.

I hate people like that. No social skills whatsoever. Make me do all the heavy lifting.

"So," I forged ahead, "I haven't been in class this week."

Nothing. Not even a "hm." I felt like hanging up right then. But I was on a mission, and the time for hanging up was last week, in my past life, not this one anymore.

I said it quickly, just to save myself any more miserable pauses. "So I was hoping you might catch me up on what I've missed if you have some time this weekend since I'm probably going back on Monday and I don't want to be totally behind and I can pay you if you want —like it's tutoring—or maybe I'll get a pizza or something—I was thinking you could come over Saturday afternoon."

A long pause. Then, "Fine. Address?"

I gave it to him and hung up before I was tempted to say anything else. Jerk. Idiot. My palms were so sweaty you'd think I had just called Prince Harry and asked him out on a date.

This had better count.

Do you hear that, great God of the gray place? I am already sacrificing for you. Not that it won't pay off, I'm sure, but do you see it isn't easy? Just because I had this Thing happen to me, doesn't mean I just jump right up and start this life all over again and I'm a completely different person and nothing is hard for me ever again.

Understand? It's hard.

And then add to that the fact that I had barely hung up when my bedroom door flew open and there was my supposed boyfriend Alex of the Massive Pecs, grinning at me like he'd given me some huge gift just by walking in.

"Hey, babe." He came over for his requisite kiss and grope.

Which he didn't realize I wasn't giving out anymore until I turned my head and nudged him off.

"Hey," he said, "what's up?" He tried again, like it had just been an oversight on my part, and I had to push him again.

He made a sound under his breath like he couldn't believe I'd just done that.

I pretended to go back to studying something off the computer screen.

I'd thought a lot about that moment—had rehearsed it in my head a hundred times while I was in the hospital—but now that it was here I wasn't sure I could pull it off. I was hyperaware of my bad leg jutting out between us. I think I thought he might kick it.

"What's going on?" he asked.

I kept my eyes on the screen. "Nothing. I just don't feel like it anymore." I clenched my hands in my lap to keep them from trembling.

"Feel like what?" he asked, even though anyone could have figured it out from the fact that I hadn't just opened my mouth wide and let him jam his tongue in there.

I used both hands to demonstrate. "No more of that."

Alex stood there for a moment, not sure if I was teasing him or not. "What're you talking about?"

"Us," I said. "Done. Over."

He still didn't get it. "What, you're pouting? Just because I didn't visit you? I told you I had double work-outs all this month. Why're you being such a bitch?"

There was no point in defending myself, no matter how tempting it was. I'd already made up my mind, and I just needed to get it over with.

"No more sex," I said plainly, finally looking him in the eye. "Ever. Never. That's it. I'm breaking up with you. We're done. Goodbye." I turned back to my screen and pretended not to care how he was looking at me.

Alex stood there for a second, and my heart was pumping like I was in the middle of a marathon, and all I could think was, *Not the leg, not the leg.* But then he grunted something and disappeared through the door.

I could relax. Which meant I could start shaking. Which I did for about the next ten minutes, wondering if he was going to come back, and what I would do if he did.

It's hard. Starting over is hard. The woman didn't tell me that. You might know what's the right thing to do, but that doesn't always make it easy. I came back with a whole list of mistakes I have to clean up, and Alex was definitely one of them.

One down, fifty million to go.

8

"So the cards decide?" I asked the woman.

"No, we decide."

The other three players had vanished moments before, and the woman and I were walking now, all alone in the gray space, nothing to see but each other. She had a body—even a sort of covering now, made out of some kind of fabric I'd never seen—and I was still just a blob of light, but that didn't seem to bother her. After a while I stopped caring about it either.

The woman paused and used her sleeve to squeegee off a section of gray in front of us, like it was dirty window.

"See that?" she asked.

I moved to where I could look past her arm and check out the view.

It was green and lush down there, like one of the displays you see at a garden store—meant to taunt you over how great your plants could grow if you only had the skill.

"What's that?" I asked.

"The world. Look here." She cleared the gray from another section, and there below were mountains capped with snow. Beautiful.

"And here." To her left was a dry, forlorn desert, with starving cattle riddled with flies.

"And here." A city jammed at rush hour, cars and people and exhaust fumes.

"So what are the cards?" I asked.

"Choices."

"But it's already decided," I pointed out. "They picked cards and got what they got. Color of skin, place of birth—"

"True, but we still have to choose."

"No." I was sort of surprised I was willing to argue with her, but why not? I was dead, I didn't really feel the need to impress anyone, and the truth was I wanted to understand. "I saw. People picked their cards and they had to take what they got. Musician, Healer, New Delhi—"

"You saw the broad outlines," the woman agreed, "but nothing of the finer details. Do you know if any of them will grow up happy? Do you know if they will lie to people, or change humanity for the good, or give up too soon, or be aborted?"

"So then what?" I asked. "If they're aborted?"

"They come back. They choose new cards. It goes on all the time. That's how the game is played. Over and over."

Gray seeped over the windows again, closing off the view. We walked in the light coming from the two of us.

"You chose Teacher," I said.

"Yes."

"But that choice was made for you. By the card."

"I accepted it," she said. "I didn't have to."

"What would happen if you didn't? If you decided no, I don't want to be some starving person in Africa or a murderer in London or whatever the cards tell you?"

"Then I wouldn't have played the game," she said. "I would have waited until I was ready."

I tried to process that. We walked along in gray and I heard snatches of what was going on below—they were charging up the defibrillator to shock my heart— and I wanted to understand so badly it was like a vise over my brain.

"You have to choose to play," I said.

"Yes."

"And that means you accept whatever cards you draw."

"Correct."

"And then you do what you can with those."

"You understand perfectly," she said. "Now let's talk about you."

She cleared the film from my own life and let me see what was going on. There I was, limp, being jolted by the paddles for the first time, and I felt so calm looking at myself that I almost wished I would die.

And I don't mean that in a bad way.

It's just that I looked so . . . peaceful. Even with all those tubes coming out of me and the blood and all the other grossness, I still looked so perfect, in a way. No struggling, no primping, no worrying, no planning, just me and my body, lying there, nowhere important to go, no speed or distance records to break, no arguments to smooth over, no effort of any kind. I either lived or I didn't. If I didn't, I'd be up there, where I already was, and that wasn't bad at all. If I lived—well, frankly it seemed like a lot of trouble at that moment to go back to. The gray place was awfully easy. All you had to do there was exist and think.

"A lot of people stay here forever," the woman said. "For that very reason. Life was too hard, and they prefer it up here. They don't want to risk the choices."

I glanced around the empty space. "Then where is everyone?"

"Different places. Some of them are alone, in their own private areas, which suits them. Some of them search for family and stay with them. It varies."

"And you?" I asked. "How long have you been here?"

"Not long. Right before you arrived."

"Is this your first time?"

She laughed. "I've lost count."

"Do you know about me? How many times—"

"I'm only guessing," she said, "but I'd say many."

"How can you tell?"

"You're talking. You're asking. You obviously want to learn and do better. The others . . . prefer not to know."

She paused and knelt down to pick up something at our feet. "Yours?" she asked, holding it up to my light.

A loose card. The ace of hearts.

"I don't know," I said. "I don't think so."

She held it up to where my heart would have been if I were covered in body and not just this naked blob. A yellow light burned out of me, like a rash spreading from where the card had touched.

She pulled the card away. "Interesting. I think you should keep this."

I held it in my stub of light. "Will you tell me what it means?"

"Yellow is for courage. I think you left it up here."

9

David Mayer smelled (surprise) of garlic.

"Hi."

"Hi."

So much for profound.

I don't know what I was expecting. Maybe I thought I'd open the door this afternoon and see David standing there, and suddenly it would all be clear. I'd understand his place in the whole scheme of things, and then I could get on with my life.

Instead it was just this awkward moment of silence while David took in his immediate surroundings: my leg, my crutches, the layout of my house.

"Where do you want to do this?" he asked.

"Uh, in here, I guess."

He followed me into the living room. The whole ten

or so steps in there I kept thinking, *"Say something, say something."* I'm not sure if I was telling him or me. I felt unreasonably shy and awkward. It was the most ridiculous thing—he's the one who should have been nervous, not me.

But David didn't get that. He opened his books and got right down to the business of calculus because that's the kind of social dumbass he is. Took no note of being alone with the second-most-popular girl at Pinedale High, seemed completely oblivious to the fact that despite my recent ordeal I looked pretty damn hot today—not that I care about that anymore, but a fact is a fact—and (further evidence of his complete cluelessness, as if we need it) pulled off his shoes and socks before plopping into the chair next to me and didn't even wonder if (a) that was cool; (b) his feet were ugly (not bad, actually); or (c) they smelled (garlic, see above).

But here's the thing:

It didn't matter. After a while I forgot all that stuff I normally would have obsessed over—crucified someone over, if I'd been around Toomy or one of my other friends—and instead just tried to see David for what he was.

His face—no, more specifically, his skin. I never noticed before—mostly because I've never sat so close and deliberately studied him—but he has skin like a baby's. He's this tall, semi-mature-looking guy—full Adam's apple, deep voice, six-foot, at least—but his skin looks as soft and pure as an infant's. I almost wanted to reach out and touch it, just to see. Wouldn't that have gotten his attention.

Or maybe not. He didn't really seem to notice me. There we were, two people who clearly did not belong in the same room together—let alone my living room—and even though I'm over trying to impress people (and certainly not David Mayer), I did go to some effort today to at least clean myself up and wash my hair. I wore a little makeup because that seemed appropriate, and I had a skirt on because it's easier with my brace and I knew I wouldn't have to worry about getting cold with our heater on full blast. I even shaved my one good leg for the first time since last week—not an easy feat.

In other words, like I said, I looked pretty damn good today, considering. Whereas David clearly made no effort at all. His hair was its usual windblown mess, he wore his daily uniform of jeans, black Converses hi-tops, white t-shirt, and gray hoodie, and it was clear from the moment he stepped into my house that he could have been there or back home napping and it would have been equally exciting for him.

So we sat there for two hours with me trying not to be too obvious about staring at him and trying to figure out why it was his face I had to see when I came back, while David barely looked at me and just kept rattling off calc problems like the machine he is.

I swear, his mind works like nothing I've ever seen. I mean, I'm smart—AP all the way—but David is on a whole other level. I understand now what sort of rewiring must have happened up in the gray space with that man who chose Mathematician. I'm surprised I didn't hear the whirring of David's brain from where I sat.

Which, if I have to be honest, was sort of exciting. To be sitting right next to someone I know without a doubt was once a bodiless soul who picked the five of clubs and then drew Pinedale, Colorado and whatever card gives you skin the texture of milk. He's a lefty, too. There must be a card for that.

We were just about wrapping it up when Beth came home from her Saturday lesson. She walked into the living room carrying her violin case and an armful of music, and froze when she saw David. Her curious eyes shifted to mine.

I made the introductions. "Music genius, meet math genius."

"Hey," Beth said.

"Hi."

Neither of them tried to deny their genius status. I approve of that. It would be a lie for either of them to pretend to be less than they are. The fact is Beth works hard to be as good as she is. Something we both have in common.

"You're eating again," Beth said happily.

"Oh. Yeah." I hadn't really noticed. At some point David and I had gotten hungry and I'd made a plate of nachos. Technically I was still in my assigned category —chips and cheese—it was the extra plate of veggie egg rolls that went too far.

Beth set her stuff down and went to the kitchen to grab a drink. She paused in the doorway, and since David had already bent over his books again, she took the opportunity to shoot me a curious look. I shook my head. But I knew she'd have questions later.

She went upstairs to practice, and David and I finished our last few problems.

We could hear music filtering down from above. I love how my sister plays. I never used to pay much attention to it—I've always had my own schedule, my own agenda—but ever since I came back I've been taking the time to listen. It's one of the things I promised myself I'd do.

David paused to listen, too. Finally—something to grab his attention. "Wow, she's really good."

"Told you." I felt this odd mixture of pride and (I hate to admit it, but) jealousy.

And also this sassy feeling of superiority for all the things I knew that genius David didn't.

Like: *Obviously Beth drew the two of hearts for this life-time. A blue spot would have shone out of her chest right before she swept down here to lodge herself in my mother's womb and wait out her time until she could be born a musical prodigy. And obviously you, David, drew the jack of clubs, so there was never any question you'd be good at math, so don't try to take any credit for it. And I—*

Right. *And I.* That's exactly what I've been lying here thinking about ever since David left.

What about me? David and Beth both know what they are, but what about me? It's something I've been wondering ever since the woman in the gray space told me I'd already drawn my cards and was already set.

Set with what?

If you'd asked me last week—if I could have even conceived of a question like that last week and thought there was such a thing as choosing cards in heaven or wherever I was and setting your life on some course from the minute you enter the womb—I would have said easily, clearly, Athlete.

Athlete. It's all I've ever wanted to be. From the first time they put me on skis when I was two. My body, I would have said as if I knew for sure, was made for movement.

Some people just know. They pick up a ball and they know. Or they run across the backyard on their chubby little toddler legs and they feel it and know it down to the core of their bones: I am an athlete. I was made for this. Please don't trouble me with any of the details of life—the schooling, the having to work for a living, the whole bothersome aspect of getting by day to day—they just know that all they ever have to do in life is go from one sporting event to another. Climb here, run there, hit this, ski down that. Wake up and go until you drop, then start all over again.

And if you asked any single person I know, they'd say the same thing about me. Toomy's dad. Any of my soccer coaches. My parents. My ski coaches. The guys at the batting cage. The people I climb with. My old water polo teammates. What haven't I done that this town has to offer?

But so what? What have all my medals and trophies and record-breaking this or that ever gotten me? And then you look at someone like David Mayer, who, despite all of his social ineptness and personality defects, at least knows what he's supposed to be doing with his life.

Do you think David lies in bed at night wondering, "Gee, should I go out for track and field this year, or take college-level calculus instead?" For that matter, do you think he gives even a second's thought to any of the stupid things I usually obsess over? You think he cares about who he goes out with, who he's seen with, what people are saying about him, what he looks like, what he wears?

Please. A guy like David makes his whole life about math—from multiplying and dividing numbers on license plates, to racing the cashier at the grocery store to see if he can add in his head faster than she can scan.

I know because it came up this afternoon in my one brief attempt at casual conversation.

Which is why a guy like David will never get a girlfriend.

Not my problem.

My problem is much, much larger. My problem is I died and found out while I was away that I have been wasting my life somehow—taking the coward's way out, if you believe the ace of hearts—and if I'm going to make any kind of sense of my future I have to figure out what I picked in my own card game back in the beginning, and now I'm pretty sure I know it wasn't Athlete.

I know this because:

1. The woman pretty much told me so.

2. She didn't need to tell me, because I somehow felt it while I watched everyone else pick their cards, but I didn't want to admit it to myself.

3. I have injured myself in so many different, destructive ways in just sixteen years, I have to think maybe my body is telling me this isn't the way it wants to go.

4. Ever since I woke up back in this body I have felt a deep, depressing longing for something that I know I do not have.

And that thing I do not have is the thing I need to get. If only I can figure out what it is.

10

The woman and I walked for a long time. Every now and then she'd swoosh away a sleeveful of gray and we'd both watch the pageant below.

Everything was so beautiful. Even war can be beautiful when there's no sound. There was a majesty to it—the way bodies fell and houses exploded and balls of light flitted upward toward us and disappeared into gray spaces of their own. I could imagine the men and women taking up their places at the card table, completely unconcerned with what had happened to them moments before, already moving ahead to their next lives and whatever they would bring.

"You said some people don't play."

"Yes," the woman answered. "They're too afraid. Or some of them are too tired."

"Have you ever . . . not played?"

"Not yet," she said. "You and I both know there's still so much to do."

I felt that. I felt the truth of what she said. Her words pulsed in me, the light burning hot around my heart.

"How does it work?" I asked. "How many lives do we get?"

"As many as we need, I suppose. Or maybe as many as we can bear."

"How many have you had?" I asked. "I mean, you said you've lost count, but how can you really tell?" What I really wanted to know was how many I had had.

"I don't know the number," the woman said. "I only know the feelings. Sometimes I hear something or see something that reminds me. Or I meet someone—like you—and I know this isn't the first time and won't be the last. Some of us are linked forever. We help each other learn, life after life. If you'd pay attention, Cara, you'd see there are teachers all around you. We keep coming back to help each other learn our lessons so we can move on."

"So you think . . . *we've* met before?" My heart—or whatever was inside me in that bodiless blob of light— sped up at the thought of it.

"Can't you feel it?" she asked. "I don't know where we've been together or how many times, but I'm certain we know each other."

The truth is I was certain, too.

And ever since I got back alive, I've been thinking about who the other ones are—the ones I've known before. My sister Beth, for sure. Maybe my mother. Definitely not my father—I barely know him in this life, let alone remember him from a past one.

Not Toomy. Not Alex. Not any of the people I used to hang out in Life Number One. They all feel like strangers. The thought of them leaves me cold.

But what about David Mayer? Now that's a weird thought. He certainly acts like he's comfortable around me, when he has no reason to be. Any other guy in his situation would have been at least somewhat nervous about coming over to my house. But maybe that doesn't mean anything. Maybe that's just David. Maybe he's just completely oblivious.

What's bizarre is that I never would have given him a moment's thought if I hadn't seen his face flit across my vision just as I woke up. I could easily have gone my whole life and never had a conversation with him.

But now that I do know him, I wonder. What if he was my brother once? Or my slave? Or the cave man in the cave next to mine? I mean, who knows how far these histories go? He could be anyone and I'll never know until I go back to the gray space and maybe meet him over a hand of cards some day.

Or maybe he's just a stranger that I'm meeting for

the first time in this Cara Campbell life, Part Two, post-death.

But whether we've met before isn't the point. I still think the woman is right: David has something to teach me.

Otherwise why would I keep thinking about him?

11

I couldn't put off school forever. Although now I wish I had.

One of the disadvantages to being a semi-celebrity like me is there's no use trying to hide. The minute my mom helped me out of her car this morning, everyone was on me. "Cara this! Cara that! Cara Dara!" Noise, noise, noise, everybody shut up. I almost begged my mother to let me get back in the car and escape home again.

But I guess it comes with the territory. I've worked hard to get where I am.

You know, David Mayer may have acted like we were all hicks when he showed up freshman year, but the truth is Pinedale High is on the map. We've won enough state championships in football, soccer, skiing, softball, baseball, and basketball to make sure of that. College recruiters have the school on speed dial. Parents uproot their families and move here on purpose to get their sport-star kids into the program.

It's why the jocks' table at Pinedale High is the most coveted spot to sit, because everyone knows we are gods. And it's why Toomy is the number one goddess. Because her father is Dale Toomy, Pinedale High School's Senior Athletic Director. He's the one who made the program what it is. Well, him, and the stars like all of us.

That's the pack I run in. Anyone looking from the outside would say it's been a good life, being me. Being second only to Toomy. Being Alex's girlfriend. Always being one of the lead dogs.

Yeah, well.

I tried today, I really did.

I made my way to our table in the cafeteria, half hating my crutches, half loving them because right away they answered everyone's question about when I'd be back in action. Anyone could see the obvious answer was "a while." No one knows the real answer is "never."

"Hey, babe, take your books?" Alex asked, already reaching for my backpack.

"No, thanks," I said, not looking at him. I straddled the bench, since it was easier than trying to swing my leg and its stiff brace under the table.

Alex leaned over to kiss me, and I had to turn away again. Get a clue.

He didn't like that one bit. "What are you doing?" he muttered so no one else could hear. Like we'd never had that conversation a few days ago.

I didn't even bother answering. I tried to ignore him, which wasn't easy with his body just centimeters from mine. I could feel the heat of anger coming off him. "*Mine. MINE.*" I was still his property—he wasn't going to let anyone see it differently, including me. At least he didn't have his arm around me. He must have gotten at least part of the message.

Toomy said, "So what're you going to do about P.E.? They going to let you hang out, or what?"

"No, Ms. Josephson gave me a note. I'm supposed to go to the library." What I didn't say was I had asked my counselor for that note.

Toomy hates Ms. Josesphson. "Lame! And do what?"

I shrugged like I didn't know. But I did know. So why lie? I promised I wasn't going to do that anymore.

So I fixed it. "Read the encyclopedia."

Toomy laughed, but then she saw I was serious. So did the other people at the table. Conversation stopped briefly, for which I was grateful, since I was already tired of talking.

Over in the far corner of the lunchroom sat David Mayer, eating some sort of pasta dish, and he was doing exactly what I wanted to be doing: sitting alone, reading a book.

Even though I'm sure he saw me come in—I mean, everybody did—I kept watching David as I hobbled to the jocks' table, to see if he'd catch my eye. He never looked up. And here I was now, still staring at him, wishing I could sit over there instead of with the gods.

But that's what this new life is about, right? Making the hard choices. I'm not supposed to live like a coward anymore. I may not know what else I'm supposed to be, but at least I know that much.

I took a deep breath, threaded my arms back into my backpack, and hoisted myself onto the crutches. "Hey, I'll talk to you later," I told Toomy, but that was a lie, so I corrected it and said, "See you later," which was undoubtedly true.

And while the conversation buzzed behind my back, and my former friends expressed their disbelief and outrage, I slowly made my way to far end of the lunchroom and took a seat at the farthest end of the table that David occupied. I wasn't looking for conversation from him—far from it. I just wanted to be away.

David glanced up briefly as I settled onto the bench, then went back to his book.

I pulled out my Spanish book, and for the rest of lunch sat there reading and practicing under my breath. And even though I knew my friends were all staring at me and talking about me and wondering what the hell was up, for the first time EVER in the history of my life at that school, I was finally doing exactly, only, completely what I wanted to do.

And oh, my God, the feeling.

I wanted to ask David, "Is this what it's like for you? Have you always been this way? Don't you love it? Why didn't you tell me?" but of course, that would have ruined everything.

The woman in the gray space told me I needed teachers. She said they were all around me. She said I would know what to do if I paid attention. She said I never paid attention.

Well, I'm paying attention now. And I'm pretty sure David Mayer has something to teach me. I don't know if it's about being alone or about being a freak and not caring what anyone thinks, or maybe it's something more profound than that. I hope so. But whatever it is, I'm going to keep hanging around David until I figure it out.

So I will continue to sit at his table, not talking to him, but also not being talked to by anyone else. No matter what the consequences.

Which, if you'd asked me a week and a half ago, I would have said was the hardest thing I'd ever had to do in my life. But I don't care anymore. I truly don't care.

Because now I understand about Time. And I know I can't afford to waste another second of it. I have spent my whole life wondering and worrying what other people think of me and want from me, and now I understand how meaningless that is.

When you're standing in the gray place, looking down on the paradise that is Earth, you don't see all the commotion of people's expectations. All you see is the beauty. All you see is what you might do in such a place, whether it's the mountains or the desert or a city filled with souls. All you see is you and what you can do. And what other people think of you or want from you is just noise. It's garbage. It's the film over the window that the woman cleared away with her sleeve.

Toomy caught up with me as I left the lunchroom. "What is wrong with you?" she said. "Why're you acting so psycho?"

I'm not psycho, I wanted to say.

You don't understand.

I've been reborn, I almost said.

Instead I kept right on lying. "I'm just tired."

12

"Hey," Beth said, holding out another five-bar selection of fancy chocolate.

"Where are you keeping all of these?"

"Secret stash." She plopped onto my bed and carefully unwrapped hers. My sister is a very tidy eater. I set my bar aside for a moment while I finished downloading an Alicia Keys song.

"So what's the deal with Alex?" Beth asked.

I kept my eyes on the computer. "What do you mean?"

"He's driven past our house about fourteen times in the last hour. He keeps slowing down, staring at our windows, then speeding up again. Did you two have a fight or something?"

I sighed. Might as well get it over with—they were

all going to find out sooner or later. "I broke up with him."

"Why?"

I could have made something up, but then I thought if I don't start telling the truth now, when will I? And Beth seemed as good a person to practice on as anyone else.

"I don't like him." Hate him is more like it, but I didn't need to go there.

"Why? What happened?"

"He . . . let's just say he's not a good guy."

I could have left it at that. But the girl did bring me chocolate. And besides, ever since our talk last week about death, I've been feeling like opening up to her. The more I think about it, I really believe it's possible Bethie and I have been through more than one life together. If that's so, I should try to make this one better than the last, right? The woman said we're all here to learn. So maybe it was the wrong decision—maybe Beth is too young to hear it—but I told her anyway.

"Because our relationship is totally about sex," I said, "and I'm not having sex anymore."

Beth's eyes grew wide. "Seriously?"

"Which part—the sex or the no sex?"

"Both. Either." She made herself comfortable, belly-down on my bed, and unwrapped another bar of chocolate. She wasn't leaving any time soon—she could tell this was going to be good.

Where do you start with a conversation like that? I was pretty sure my mother hadn't handled it with Beth yet—she still hasn't gotten around to it with me.

"You'll understand some day," I said. "Sex isn't what you think it is. It's *way* more personal than it looks on TV. It's . . . intrusive. You're . . . exposed. And I don't just mean naked exposed, I mean . . . personally. Mentally. If you can't trust the guy it really sucks. He's seen you, he's touched you—you've given away a part of you. It's hard to explain."

"But, is it . . . good?" Beth almost whispered. I think she was afraid I would stop talking if she interrupted. "Do you like it?"

Why not be honest? "Parts of it. I like the touching. It feels good sometimes when he does it a certain way. But now he's too rough—I haven't liked it for a long time."

"When did you start?" Beth asked.

"Last spring. Right after my birthday. I decided sixteen was old enough—*big* mistake. You should wait until you're at least eighteen—or even later."

Beth scoffed.

"I'm serious, Bethie. Promise you'll come talk to me first—you really need to think it through. It sucks to make a mistake. Don't be one of those idiots who say, 'Oh, one thing led to another, and next thing I knew—' No. There's no 'one thing leads to another.' You always know what's going to happen. You really have to be ready mentally—it changes you. Not to mention you'd better have all your birth control in order—none of this 'whoops' bullcrap. I'll help you with all that when it's time. But you have to promise me you'll come talk to me before you even head down that road with anyone. You promise?"

Beth rolled her eyes. "Fine. Whatever." I could tell she was embarrassed, but too bad. If she couldn't hear it from me, she wasn't ready to think about any of it anyway. I really hate these girls who act like it's never going to happen, so they never think through their plan, and next thing you know they're having babies in the bathroom at school.

"So . . ." she said, "what was it like, the first time? I mean, if you don't mind me asking." She kept her gaze on the thread she was picking from my bedspread.

I blew out a breath. Now I was kind of embarrassed, too. I don't usually talk about my sex life with anyone— not even Toomy, although she's been plenty graphic with me about hers—but I figured if Beth had the guts to ask, I might as well have the guts to answer.

"It was . . . exciting. Thrilling. Dangerous-feeling. Because I knew what was going to happen that night, but Alex didn't. I knew he always had condoms with him—you have to absolutely make sure of that, Bethie

—either he has to have one or you do. No exceptions. You understand?"

Beth nodded.

"I made sure I was already on the Pill for a few weeks, even though I didn't tell Alex. Then I picked the night, and when he got to a certain point—the point where I usually always made him stop—I just let him just keep on going. And boy, was he a happy man."

"I bet."

"He'd been after it for a long time. Now I wish I'd never given in. It was stupid."

"Did you . . . love him?"

"I thought so. But now I just think I went along with the whole thing, you know? Good-looking guy, popular, we're so perfect together, blah, blah. You know?"

Beth nodded and was quiet for a moment. "Do you think maybe he loved you, though?"

"Nope. Never. I think it was always about sex."

"Wow. That sucks."

"You have no idea."

Beth gathered up her chocolate wrappers, and I figured that was it for today's sisterly truth session. But Beth still had one more question up her sleeve.

"So what's the deal with that David guy? Is he going to be your new boyfriend?"

She caught me off guard. I answered automatically. "No, David Mayer is a freak, thank you very much."

"No, he's not!" Beth said, laughing. "I think he's cute."

"Compared to the boys in eighth grade, I'm sure that's true."

"He has a nice face," she persisted. "And a nice mouth."

And nice skin, I could have said.

"So what's wrong with him?" Beth wanted to know.

"Oh, just his personality, his attitude, the fact that he barely speaks—"

"He was talking to you," Beth said. "I heard him."

"Math," I said. "He was speaking Math. That's not normal."

"You were speaking Math back." Beth came over to gather up my chocolate wrappers and repo the last two uneaten bars. "I still say he's cute."

I rolled my eyes. "You'd better clear all your future boyfriends through me. I question your judgment."

Beth left, but her question lingered on: *So what's wrong with him?*

Honestly? Everything. It's one thing to brave leaving the jocks' table to go sit with him like I did today, but let's not get carried away. I may have come back different, but I'm still me. And even though I know for certain I'm not supposed to be with Alex anymore, it doesn't mean I go to the complete opposite side of the spectrum and start dating someone like David.

I'm not dating, period. I know every single person at

my high school—in this town, for that matter—and there's not a single one of them I can even imagine wanting to spend time with.

Let alone sharing my body with. Because that's what it's always going to be from now on, isn't it? I doubt I'll ever be able to go back to being someone like Beth, still innocent, still getting so excited over the prospect that a boy might actually kiss me. From now on it's probably always going to be about sex. And I'm sorry, but I just don't feel like it anymore. Alex ruined that for me.

So let's say the unthinkable happened, and I actually started to like David Mayer *that way*. As impossible as that is to envision. Forget the fact that Alex would never let it go. Forget that Toomy and the rest of the gods would make it their business to torture David and me daily. Those are the good parts. Those are the ones I could take.

What I can't take is the way I know I'd feel about it: like I'd fooled myself into thinking I liked him, just to prove that I was different now. Maybe I shouldn't say that, but being honest means being honest with myself. And I know me. I have certain standards. A guy has to look a certain way. Have a certain level of . . . clout. Alex may be a total pig, but at least he had some power. And I liked being part of that.

Although it's also the thing that made me afraid to break up with him back when I knew I should have. It took a pretty serious jolt to get me to do it. So maybe that whole power thing is the last criterion I should be looking for.

I think the easiest thing to do is to stay away from all of them. Declare myself off limits until I can graduate and get out of this town. Find new people—people who don't know me now or how I used to be—and start over.

That's what I need—to start over.

And that means alone.

13

They had already shocked my heart once. I actually felt it a little, somewhere on the surface of my lump of light.

The woman said, "They're trying so hard, aren't they?"

"Yes, I think so."

"It's nice that they want you around."

We came to a bench, like a park bench, stuck there in the middle of gray space with no view backwards or forwards. We sat.

I looked at her. She had lovely eyes, light brown like a paper bag, and thick brown hair that grew halfway down her back. I have no idea how old she was—could have been thirty, could have been less or more. Her mouth naturally turned up into a smile. Not everyone's does. My mother's mouth is so straight across if she's not smiling all the time people think she's mad.

"So," the woman said, "what do you think you'll do?"

"What do you mean?" I asked.

"Death changes all of us, no matter how briefly we're gone. Now you have a chance to start over. What do you want to do differently?"

Oh, my God, what a question. For all the times in my life I'm sure I've thought, *"Why did I do that? Can't I rewind?"* I couldn't in that moment think of the right answer to give her. Of course I had made mistakes—who hasn't?—but it doesn't mean you can answer off the top of your head, "Cara Campbell, you're about to come back from the dead, what are you going to change first?"

I began with the obvious: "I should probably be nicer," and that seemed to go over all right, so I kept going. "And pay more attention to my little sister, I guess. And not lie so much."

And then I was on a roll.

"And break up with Alex—that whole thing was a huge mistake. And stop worrying so much about what people think of me. And be nicer to people."

"You mentioned that."

"Well, it's probably my biggest flaw. I just blow off people who I don't think are—" I hesitated, because it was an ugly thing to say.

"Try being honest," the woman prompted.

"Who aren't as good as I am."

"In your opinion," she said.

"Right. And also in the opinion of my friends. Some of them can be pretty harsh." I hesitated. "Which is kind of the problem."

"Because?"

"Because it might be hard . . ." I sighed and just gave in. If I was going to tell her the truth I might as well tell all of it. "Because then they'll turn on me and be that mean to me."

"The coward's fear," she said.

"Yes."

The woman poked me where my chest would have been. "But you have the card." The yellow light from the ace of hearts radiated outward from her finger. "Remember that."

"Clear!"

I turned at the sound. "Am I going back?"

"Soon. I want to ask you something, Cara. What do you think you are meant to do in this life?"

I don't see how it's possible, considering I didn't have any glands, but I swear I started to sweat. "I don't know."

"We all know," she said. "I'd like you to go back remembering what it is you meant to do."

Now I was feeling sick. Like someone had trapped me inside a little room and the air was running out.

"Don't be afraid," she said. "This is what you came

back for. You've forgotten what you meant to do, and you need to remember."

Oh, God. It was killing me. You know how it hurts sometimes to hear someone be brutally honest? A part of you likes that you're hearing the pure, absolute truth, but the rest of you—most of you—just can't stand it. It's so unnatural. You want the person to go back to being fake, where it's safe and everyone knows their lines.

But there's no way this spirit or angel or almost-reincarnated being was going to let me off the hook. I could see the intensity, the light coming from her eyes, and I knew that even if the doctors down below got my heart up and running, the woman would hold me there on that park bench until I'd given her a straight answer.

"Cara," she said, "be still. Just answer from your heart."

"I have to change the world." And right as I said it, I knew that it was true.

"Yes, but how?" she wanted to know.

"I have to tell the truth."

14

My second try at school, post-mortem.

"What's going on?" Toomy asked me this morning. I had tried to sneak past everyone on my way to class, but no go. It's hard when you're so slow. "Why're you acting so stoned?"

"I don't know," I lied. "Guess I just have a lot on my mind."

"Yeah? Does that include how you blew us all off yesterday?" she asked angrily. "Your boy is wondering what the hell—"

"Listen," I interrupted, "I don't have time right now. It takes me a long time to get to class."

Lies, lies, lies. Telling the truth is great in theory, but hardly ever practical in real life.

But then later, as I was heading in for lunch, she

grabbed my arm and I just didn't have the guts to shake her off. She escorted me to the table—"our" table—and I sat there and took it and I HATE that about myself. I am weak. I admit it.

"You're so f—ing hot," Alex murmured as he crowded against me on the bench. "C'mon, babe, I miss you. What do I have to do? I can't stand it anymore. You're f—ing driving me crazy."

God!!!! Did I not say clearly enough it's over? And stop calling me babe—I've always hated that.

But what did I do—tell him off? Get up and leave? Do even the slightest thing to help myself? No. I sat there, coward that I am. I let him tell me things. Whisper things to me. I let him think . . . I don't know what he thinks. That we're back together, I suppose. That he can come over tonight after everyone is asleep and I'll just let him in and it's back on.

As we walked out Toomy took me aside and said, "Thank God. I thought you were losing it. Sitting with that asswipe Mayer?"

I glanced back over my shoulder. David was sitting where I wanted to be. Where I was supposed to be, if I weren't such a coward.

I don't deserve this second life.

15

"Um, David," I said, doing my best to hobble up to him as he headed for his car after school.

He turned to me, but didn't say anything. Not that I expected him to.

"I could still use some help," I said.

He glanced down at my leg.

"I mean with calc. I'm still so far behind—"

"You said something about paying me," he interrupted.

"Oh. Okay."

"You don't have to pay me."

"Oh," I said. "Okay." The guy is simply incomprehensible.

He glanced at my leg again. "Need a ride?"

"My mom's . . ." I checked my watch. I could still

catch her. "Yeah, if you don't mind. Let me just call her. I'm sure she'd rather keep working."

His car is a two-door Mercury. Not the best situation for someone whose leg is in a brace. Finally we worked out me reclining in back with my bad leg on the seat and the good one hanging on the floor. Not exactly the luxury of my mother's Mercedes wagon, but I didn't care. I had to salvage at least one iota of my life today, and this was my only shot.

I hate that I thought this, but I felt a fleeting moment of relief that Alex and Toomy were at practice already and wouldn't see me getting into David Mayer's car. I have to stop caring about that.

We didn't talk on the way home. Big surprise. He didn't play any music, either. It was just this weird, uncomfortable ride—in more ways than one—and when he pulled up to my house he just turned off the engine and sat facing forward.

"I hate to ask," I said, "but can you give me a hand out?"

"Sure." He got out and opened the passenger door and helped me.

And here's what I noticed: If it had been Alex, he would have swooped me into his arms to show me how strong he is, and he would have carried me all the way inside even if I told him not to, and we would have ended up in my bedroom, and it would either be a big fight to get him out or I'd give in and we'd be naked on my bed.

But David isn't strong. David wouldn't even know how it is you get a girl from the car into bed within a matter of minutes. David is completely clueless, which is why he helped me out gently, not saying anything, but making sure he never bumped my leg or hurt me in any way.

I leaned against the car while he got my crutches. And I have to admit I liked him just then. Not *liked* him —I'm through with that for a long, long time—but liked him as a human being.

Liked him enough to mean it when I said, "Thanks a lot. That's really nice." And liked him enough to say, "I really will pay you, if you want."

"No." Then he just stood there, silent and waiting. For what? I've never been around someone so comfortable not talking—even if it makes other people, like me, very uncomfortable.

"Um, so do you want to go over some calc now?" I asked. "We've got food. Is this a good time?"

He shrugged. He pulled my backpack out of the car then got his own, and followed me into the house.

I don't get him. At all. We sat at the kitchen table eating nachos again, and I didn't catch him looking at me even once. He sat there at my table already doing some of his own homework while he waited for me to get mine out.

SUPERFREAK.

And I don't know what got into me. I really don't. Maybe it's because I hadn't been honest a single second of today up until then, and I just felt like seeing what would happen. Or maybe I just wanted to shake him up a little, to see if he ever reacts to anything.

"Do you ever think about sex?" I asked.

He kept right on writing out problems. "Yes."

"With me?"

Didn't even look up. "Yes."

Okay, so at least he was somewhat human. And maybe not so oblivious after all. "What if I don't want to have sex with you?"

"I didn't think you did."

I was just about to come up with some sort of witty reply—I have no idea what—when Beth came home and found us in the kitchen.

"Hey."

"Hey."

I've noticed David doesn't look me in the eye very often, but right then he was—staring right at me, brown eyes to green, and I couldn't tell what I saw there. Anger? Curiosity? Amusement? Whatever it was, it was unnerving.

And I have to admit that in that moment, just for a second—

No, no I don't.

16

I looked away just to escape his eyes, and David started chatting with Beth like I wasn't even in the room. But then when she grabbed her snack and went upstairs to practice he returned his attention to me.

"Why did you ask me that?" he said.

"Ask you what?" Although of course I knew.

He wasn't playing my game. He just kept looking at me with a calm expression, waiting for me to break.

"I don't know," I said. "Just for fun."

"You think it's fun to pry into people's lives when you have absolutely no business there?"

"No." Jeez. Lighten up. I cracked a smile, mainly because he was making me so nervous.

"What if I had asked you those same questions?" he demanded. "Wouldn't you have been offended?"

"Yes."

"All right then." He started gathering up his books.

"Wait—so you're mad at me?" I asked.

"No." But he kept shoving his stuff into his backpack.

"David, hold on." I gripped his wrist. "I'm sorry. I didn't mean to offend you."

I've never had someone look at me so directly—like he wasn't afraid of letting me see into him the way he was trying to see into me.

"Why did you call me last week?" he asked. "What was the point?"

"Because . . ."

And here it was again. A chance to make a choice.

The truth? *I died and when I came back to my body I thought about you. So I wanted to figure out why that was. Ha, ha. Weird, huh?*

No, the real truth:

I died and I thought about you. I don't know why I died or why I came back or why I would ever think about you for even a second, but I'm trying to solve all those mysteries, and you're one of them.

I went with:

"I told you—I need help with calc."

"No, you don't, and you know it. So tell me why."

I couldn't take the way he was looking at me—too open and honest and unnerving. "Okay, fine. It's because I think you're really an interesting person, David. And that's the truth."

"So you're interested in me? As in dating?"

I laughed, and realized a second too late he wasn't trying to be funny.

He zipped his backpack closed. "I think we're done here." He shouldered his pack and headed for the door.

"Wait—that's it?" I fumbled for my crutches and followed. "David, wait!"

He turned on the porch and gave me a tired gaze. "I knew this was a mistake. I shouldn't have even come the first time."

"Then why did you?" I challenged. This wasn't going at all the way I planned.

He shrugged. "Boredom. Curiosity."

At least that was something I could work with. "Aren't you still? Curious?"

"No, I've pretty much seen what I came to see. You're exactly what I expected."

"Which is what?" This guy was seriously starting to irritate me.

"You're boring."

"I'm *boring*?" Of all the insults that least applied—

"I think you're incredibly arrogant and self-centered," David said, "and that's boring."

Unbelievable. I slumped onto my crutches. This whole thing was a disaster. Just because I had to open my mouth and ask him about his sex life.

"You really don't like me, do you?" I asked, not actually wanting to hear the answer.

"Nope."

It might have been nicer if he hadn't answered so quickly. "So, what," I said defensively, "you hate me?"

"No. No more than the rest of the clones."

"Why? What did we ever do to you?" Although I knew very well. "Look," I said, hurrying to cut him off just in case he did answer, "I'm not like that anymore. I swear."

"Really?" he said. "I hadn't noticed. What happened? Personality makeover?"

"No, I just don't feel the way I used to about things."

"Oh, yeah?" he answered, clearly just as bored as he'd said. "Since when?"

"Since my operation."

David gazed up at the porch roof and shook his head. "Cara . . ."

Finally, maybe some sign that I was getting to him.

But instead all he finished with was, "Good luck." Then he stepped off the porch and continued heading for his car.

"That's it? Wait!" I took the steps faster than I should have, and chased after him.

David threw his pack into the car and turned to me. "I don't know even know why you asked me here. What was the point of all this, Cara?"

"I don't know, maybe I'd just like us to be friends."

"Yeah. Maybe you would. I just don't happen to believe it."

I was losing what little chance I had to make any sense out of why he was supposed to be in my life. "What if I sat with you at lunch?"

David chuffed. "What if you did? Am I supposed to feel honored?" He got into his car and slammed the door.

Time for a desperation move, even if it gave him the wrong impression. I leaned in through the window. "Do you have a girlfriend?"

"None of your business." He turned the key in the ignition.

"David—" I knew I had lost him. Somewhere between "do you think about having sex with me?" and laughing when he asked if I was interested in him, I had lost.

"I'm sorry," I said, and that was the truth. "I didn't do this right."

"Do what right?"

"Try to become friends with you."

The engine was running, but at least it was still in park. David tapped the steering wheel with his thumb and gazed out the front windshield. "So that's what this was about? You're collecting a new entourage? You need more people to fawn over you?"

"I think you're an interesting person," I said again. "I'd like to get to know you."

"Tell me why."

"I just did. I think you're an interesting—"

He turned to me, eyes fully on mine. "No, Cara. Tell me *why*."

At some point you have to stop acting like a coward if you ever want to get any better.

I took a deep breath.

"I died during the operation and went to heaven or someplace like it, and when I came back into my body I was thinking of you, and I'd like to know why that is."

His eyes narrowed. "Excuse me?"

I sagged on my crutches. "Don't make me say it again."

"You had an NDE?"

"A what?"

"Near-death experience," he snapped. "Is that what you're telling me?"

"I don't know. I guess—"

"I don't believe this." He gunned the motor and left.

17

I was right about Alex. Because I was weak at lunch today, he took that as an invitation.

Two in the morning, pebbles against my window. That's supposed to mean I sneak downstairs, unlock the door, take him silently into the family room or out to our shed, shut the door, take off all my clothes, and get right to it.

It's supposed to mean nothing has changed, I haven't changed, nothing happened to me two weeks ago, I haven't learned anything.

But I have learned something. Not enough, but something.

I ignored him for as long as possible, but he wasn't going away. It's not so easy to sneak downstairs when you're on crutches, but I managed. I took it as a personal challenge.

Opened the door. "What?"

He grinned. "Come on. It's freezing out here."

I didn't move. "Alex, go home. I'm not doing this anymore."

He slipped his hand around my waist and went in for the neck kiss.

I pushed him off. "I'm serious. This is over. I don't know how many ways I have to say it. We. Are. DONE."

He frowned. "What're you so mad about?"

"I'm not mad—" *You IDIOT.* "—I just don't want to go out with you anymore. Sorry—" *No, not sorry.* "—but you're just going to have to accept that."

He stood there in the cold light of the moon trying to stare me down.

"Good night." I started to close the door.

"Just jerk me off," he murmured, starting to undo his pants.

"Are you kidding me?"

He came toward me again and this time I pushed him hard.

"Mom?" I shouted, "Dad?"

"Shut the f— up!" Alex snapped, but at least he started doing up his pants. "What is with you, you f— ing bitch?"

I laughed so he wouldn't know I was scared. "I don't love you."

"So what?"

"Okay," I said. "Right. Goodbye." And this time he let me shut the door. I moved away from it, like I thought he might shoot me through the wood.

He gave the door one solid bang with his fist, just to prove he was still in charge, but then a few moments later I heard his car door slam and saw the lights through the window as he drove away.

When I turned around, my mother was on the stairs.

"Want to tell me what's going on?"

I hiked my armpits back on top of my crutches. "Nothing. Just Alex. I broke up with him."

"Is everything all right?"

"Yeah. I guess so." I hobbled past her and started up the stairs.

"Honey, if you want to talk—"

"I know, Mom. Thanks."

I did want to talk. But not to her.

I waited until I thought she was back asleep, then went in to wake up Beth.

I didn't realize before what a relief it is for someone to know your secrets. And I happen to have the best audience of all in my own house. Beth is like me—she craves information. And I didn't realize before tonight that it feels equally good to give it out. I could have gone back to bed, but having told Beth part of the story already, I felt responsible for telling her the rest.

"He really said that?" she asked when I reported Alex's parting request.

"Yep."

"What a pig!"

"You got it."

Which gave me the chance to repeat the warning I'd already given her: Be sure he's the right guy. Be sure he's nice. Cute isn't everything—in fact, cute is usually a drawback. Guys think they can get by on their looks, just like girls do. You have to take your time. Be sure. There's never any rush.

How did I get so wise? How did I go from being the stupid idiot in the middle of this mess, to becoming this mature beacon of wisdom just a few weeks later?

I finally left her room when it looked like Beth was about to pass out. I was tired, too, but not ready to go to sleep. Time stretches out like a line, and if I miss a few hours of rest now and then, I don't think it will affect me in the long run.

What will affect me is going back to the way I was. I was weak today—well, yesterday now. I let my old life suck me back in. I forgot who I'm supposed to be.

But today will be different. Today I'm going to remember. I was different up there. I knew what I didn't know before. I have a mission, and though I'm not fully sure what it is yet, I know what it is not.

It is not living the same stupid unconscious life I've lived for sixteen years. It is not doing what other people want me to do just so I can make them happy. It's not sitting at a table with a dozen people who might be fine for someone else but are definitely not fine for me.

It is boldly sitting with David Mayer at lunch because something in my soul tells me I need him to be my friend. And it's ignoring whatever looks I will get and whatever snide remarks people will make, because Time is a line stretching forever, and what happens today or tomorrow at Pinedale High is so unbelievably insignificant not only to my life but to the total span of Time stretching from now until forever from earth into the gray.

Okay, now I'm tired. My alarm goes off in an hour.

Repeat after me: I don't care what they say. I don't care what they say.

Pick up the ace of hearts and hold it.

18

Those makeover shows always give us the thrill of watching homely girls become great beauties. They learn how to dress, how to pluck their eyebrows so they don't look like cave women, how to walk, do their makeup, everything.

What do you do if you want the opposite? I already am the beauty—I'm not being conceited, it's just true. If I'm supposed to tell the truth in this life, then it has to include this: I am a really pretty girl.

I have a nice body. Five-foot nine. Muscular arms and thighs from doing sports all my life. A flat stomach. Nice breasts, nice butt. A pretty face. Thick blond hair that looks good whether it's down and combed or up in a sloppy ponytail like I don't care about it. Well, I do care—or at least I did—because I knew the effect I have on people. They like to look. These are just the facts.

I'm smart, too, or at least I know how to work hard in school and always get the grades. I am the daughter any parent would pay to have. I don't smoke, don't drink, don't do drugs. Yes, I've had sex, but I made sure I was on the Pill first and I always made Alex wear a condom because I knew I wasn't his first.

I go to church with my parents on the requisite occasions, Easter and Christmas. I cheerfully attend every family function where daughters are required: office picnics, Take Our Daughters and Sons to Work Day, vacations with my cousins and aunt and uncle, all of Beth's recitals.

I don't talk back. I chew with my mouth closed. I spray the bathroom if I've stunk it up. I've never shoplifted, never stolen money from my parents. I keep my room clean, help with the dishes, remember my parents' birthdays and always get them a gift.

Not to mention all those shelves in the living room devoted to my many trophies and ribbons and victory photos. A real superstar.

Fairly perfect, right?

Then why, when I was up there reviewing my life with some stranger who probably wasn't actually a stranger, why did I know right away that what I had been for sixteen years wasn't good enough, and I needed to undergo some radical changes if I was going to be worthy of this life?

Because it's like I told her: I'm mean. I am the most uncharitable person I know. I don't cut anyone any slack. If you don't measure up, you're dog shit, and I'm sorry but that's just the truth. I've surrounded myself with people who think the same way, and we are an impenetrable wall of criticism and ridicule, ready to take on anyone who would dare try to be less cool than we are.

God.

I wish there were a book or a movie out there that showed the step-by-step transformation of someone like me into the plain, sweet girl who maybe doesn't know how to dress right or do her hair, but God her heart is pure, and we love her just for that.

And maybe she ends up with some simple, plain-looking guy who grows his own food or works in a soup kitchen or counsels suicide patients or does something else noble.

And they go off together in their fantasy world where they think the best of everyone and assume everyone else is doing the same. If people are laughing at them, they can't hear it. Everything is perfect.

I'll admit I've thought about it a few times: me and David. Thought about it in vivid detail, as a matter of fact, and I'm sorry, but I just don't see it. I'd like to think I could change so much inside that being with someone like him wouldn't feel like such an incredible step down. I'd like to believe that someday I could meet some guy and see his soul first, not whether he's got a decent haircut or is wearing the right clothes and knows how to fit in. I'd like to think that, but I'm not there yet. I might never be.

I think I need to go into the Peace Corps. Go someplace dirty and uncivilized. Live in a hut. Drink dirty water. Eat with my hands. Get used to being around people who are so poor they may die tomorrow because they don't have food. Let the experience wear on me, and come back to my parents and my country a different, almost holy person.

That kind of person could be with David. In fact, that person would ask him to come along. We might need his brains over in Calcutta or wherever they sent me.

I sat across from him at lunch today while the jocks' table buzzed and all eyes were on me, and David and I didn't talk and that was fine. Neither of us brought up what happened yesterday, when he just drove off and left me after my confession. But I figured if he didn't want me sitting with him he would have said so, so there I was.

He read a book and ignored me, I did homework and ignored him. But I sat across from him, not at the other end of the table like before. Progress, right? I might save my soul after all.

"Can you come over this weekend?" I asked him.

"No."

"Come on, David. Please? Just to hang out."

"Busy," he said.

"Fine, then I'll come to you. Where do you live?"

He just shook his head.

"It's easy to find out. I found your phone number."

"Wicked for you. You're not invited."

But I'm not giving up. David Mayer is not the hardest challenge I've ever faced in my life.

He doesn't know who he's dealing with.

19

It's Friday, and I've spent five days of sixth period doing nothing but reading the encyclopedia. I wasn't kidding about that. I figure that's a better use of my time than P.E. used to be. And look—I'm already up to *Barlow's disease (see Scurvy)*. Okay, so I've skimmed a little, but I'm still going to be very disciplined about this. I can't just skip ahead to the S's, so *(see Scurvy)* will have to wait.

This self-study isn't bad at all. I wouldn't mind ditching all my classes and just spending the whole day in the library—think of how far I'd get in the encyclopedia that way. Or I could design my own program of reading all the classics—Shakespeare, Einstein, Newton, Plato—learn from true geniuses, instead of

Pinedale High's stellar faculty. Wouldn't that be a better use of my time?

I mean, what's the point of school anyway? For me, I mean. When I was up in the gray space, you think I gave even a moment's thought to whether I'd aced that AP History test the week before? Or whether I'd gotten all my AP Chem homework right? All I cared about when I was up there was the big picture—what I've done with my life so far and what I'm supposed to do with it next. That's the only thing that really matters.

So why am I sitting here reading *Barn is a farm building used to house livestock and to store hay*? Because I said I would. And even though no one else cares about that ridiculous commitment, I do. Because that's how I am.

Which is why I need to change.

The truth is, I don't really care about school. I've never stressed about getting into college, because the coaches have always told me I'll get a full ride someplace. The only stress is deciding whether I want to go someplace that offers scholarships for skiing or for softball. And I've always known—or at least thought I knew, until recently—that after college I was going into professional sports of some kind, so what difference would a few Bs in high school make?

It's just that I can't participate in something and not want to be the best at it. So I've always knocked myself out at school just for the sake of excelling—because even though I might never beat someone like David Mayer in class standing, there's still a whole field of other people I'm consistently ahead of. And that's always mattered.

But up in the gray space, it didn't matter at all. And that's what I'm trying to stay focused on.

So I've been trying an experiment. For the last couple of days I've deliberately forced myself to slack off. Because I think the only way I'm going to ever be able to retrain myself not to be so psycho-competitive about school is to force myself not to care.

Believe me, it's not easy. At times it's killed me not to raise my hand when the answer is so obvious. And even though I'm up on all my homework, I've forced myself not to turn it in on time—and believe me, that's hard. Baby steps. I know this whole retraining will take time—like Coach Liebert making me completely overhaul my turns on the slalom course last year—but I know it will be worth it. I need to think and act differently.

Barn owl. See Owl (Important owls)—there's a category for "important owls"?

Baby steps.

Right now Toomy is probably in the weight room working on her abs and I don't care. It's been two days since the big Lunch Table Rebellion, and she isn't speaking to me, and I don't care.

No, I do care—I'm happy.

It's been easier than I thought. People are really good at hating you when you turn on them. I thought I was going to have to have all these uncomfortable conversations—*"No, it isn't you, it's me"*—but not a single one of my former friends has tried to talk to me.

They talk *at* me sometimes. "Bitch," "psycho," "loser," blah, blah, blah. "Ho bitch" (Alex's favorite), probably a bunch of others I haven't had the pleasure of hearing yet.

If you can get to the point where you just don't care about the nasty looks they're giving you, it's a sweet spot. Like finding the perfect balance over your skis on a bump run.

And that's been the key for me—treating it like a sporting event. Once I figured that out, I was golden.

Here, on crutches, wearing her least-fashionable sweats and one of her dad's ugliest T-shirts, is today's competitor, Cara Campbell the Sequel, running the seven-hour Apathy Loop through Pinedale High, and oh! she nearly fell there—that evil eye from Victoria Toomy packs a wicked punch—but she's up! She's going! She's . . . made it!!!

My other sporting event? Getting David to invite me to his house. He is a tough competitor.

I handled the address problem by getting it off the Web. I now know that his parents own their house at 4925 Lambert Avenue. I also know that she is Ginny and he is Dr. Mark Mayer. Further searches proved fruitful: He had a psychiatry practice in Denver, and she was a lawyer there. That must have been bucks. They each contributed $2,000 to the democratic candidate in the last presidential election. They both signed an on-line petition demanding more funding for national parks. If I looked a little longer I probably could have found out what color bras Mrs. Mayer buys.

"I can just show up," I threatened David. "Then what would you do?"

He gave me a bored look. "Call security."

But the truth is I don't want to just show up, I want him to ask me. It's a matter of pride. I do not want to stalk the unstalkable. I don't think humiliation is really part of this whole transformation.

I overheard Toomy today (mainly because she wanted me to overhear her) talking about how Alex is taking Kimberly to the Toomys' Halloween party tomorrow night. Whatever. I'm sort of surprised Toomy didn't snatch him up herself. She's always had a hankering for my man.

Let them all have each other. Let them swim in each other's slime. I just want to be rid of all of them. It looks like I'm doing a good job.

If David doesn't invite me over this weekend, I'm going to hang out with Beth and make her watch a bunch of stupid movies with me. I'll even make us some popcorn, even though that's not on my food list. Maybe cheesepopcorn.

Actually, my food list has expanded somewhat. I've

added in some fruit. I can't handle vegetables right now —too crunchy, too colorful—but an occasional banana or orange hasn't killed me.

My dad grilled steaks last night and they nearly did me in. I couldn't even look at them. I don't know how I used to eat that stuff. All that blood and death.

I want to know what David Mayer eats that always makes him smell like garlic. Yes, obviously he eats garlic, but I want to know in what. I know the guy's vegetarian—he made that clear when I brought out the egg rolls last Saturday and he made me show him the package to prove there wasn't any meat in them (he is way too suspicious of me). I want to know if he eats regular vegetarian food like tofu and beans, or something more exotic. Garlic Shanghai, or something like that.

I wonder what his parents are like. I couldn't find any pictures of them on the internet. There are plenty of pictures of me—the local newspaper loves me. None of David.

I should probably go back to the encyclopedia now. Or maybe I'll just sit here and stare at some trees. Life was a lot easier when that's all I did.

Maybe I'll write a blackmail note: *"David—invite me to your house or I'll tell everyone—"*

Tell everyone what?

And who's everyone? I don't have any friends anymore.

This is all working out, right? I'm doing a good job. I wanted to be alone and I am.

Great.

20

It's Saturday morning and I'm bored.

Bored out of my flippin' MIND.

Okay, I have to admit something: my experiment is a spectacular failure. This morning I woke up in a semi-panic over all the homework I didn't turn in the last two days. And I'm still agonizing over that number of protons answer I forced myself not to blurt out. I can't live like this. The simple truth is I can't *not* excel. It makes me crazy not to try.

You know what else is making me crazy? This whole immobility thing. AARRRGGG! I hate my stupid brace, I hate my stupid leg, I hate that all I can do when I'm at home is sleep, read, listen to music, play on the Internet, and think up new ways to serve cheese.

I. AM. BORED.

This is me—the me who's used to spending half my waking hours running, jumping, climbing, throwing— me. That me is starting to be one antsy, miserable person.

Fall has been late this year, but now it's really here. I can almost smell the snow. Last year we didn't get our first big storm until the day after Christmas, but I think this year it might come by Thanksgiving.

Not that it will do me any good.

I've been fooling myself. I think I thought I wouldn't mind so much being out of commission for the next few months. Even before what happened during the operation, I had all these big plans for myself so I wouldn't feel the way I feel right now. I thought I'd rent a bunch of movies, catch up on some reading, keep four steps ahead on my homework, maybe figure out how to knit.

What a joke.

There's this little motor in me that has been idle for the last few weeks, but now I can feel it humming again and IT WANTS ACTION.

It feels the crispness in the air and says, *"Run. Go run."* It tells me to hit the weight room extra hard and build up my quads so I can tear down the slopes the split-second the ski area opens again. It's telling me to go find a guy—I know, I know—because even though the whole thing with Alex was a disaster, it was still fun sometimes to feel the way my body felt.

I like my body. I can't help it. I like to see what it can do. I like to feel it in action.

The motor in me says, *"We can rebuild this knee. Stop being such a lazy pig. Forget what the doctors say. Get out there and rehab it. Since when do we take it easy?"*

Well, since we came back from the dead, that's when. I'm supposed to be spending my time figuring out what I should really be doing with my life—not going back to being exactly who I was before.

Up in the gray space, I was running out of time. I could feel it. In an operating room down here on earth my heart was getting ready to beat again. Maybe not in that second, but soon enough, and I needed to find out all I could before I went tumbling back.

The woman stretched out her long legs and leaned back on the bench like she had all the time in the world. I sat on the edge, so anxious I could have jumped out of my skin if I had any. Her questions made me nervous: "What are you going to change? What will you do differently? What do you think you're meant to do with your life?"

"Change the world," I had answered, but okay, so now what? "Change it by telling the truth." Great, but what does that mean?

It seems like if you pick the Astronaut card, or Missionary, or Movie Star, you'd know what path to walk. You'd go get this certain kind of schooling, move to Cape Canaveral or Africa or Hollywood, do this series of things, and suddenly you'd be there. Ta da! You are who you set out to be.

But Truth Teller is not a career. So there must be something else. Yesterday I kept flipping through the encyclopedia thinking I might stumble on it. Oh, *Ballistics Expert*—of course. *Banker. Bard. Bartender.*

Beth has it so easy. All she had to do once she picked her card—two of hearts—was come down to earth and bide her time until her fingers were long and strong enough to manage the violin. Ever since then, she's had no reason to doubt. She doesn't have to worry about whether she's fulfilling her purpose, because she can't help but do that. She lives for music. It's in her head constantly. Every time she plays a note, she is who she set out to be.

If I had picked Athlete, which I know now I didn't, then it would have been the same for me. From the very start I lived, ate, and breathed sports. And I would have kept on going down that road if not for the abrupt detour of being snatched out of my body, brought up to heaven or wherever, and given a good talking to. I'm grateful for the correction, but it doesn't mean I know what to do now.

What do I do now?

Did I mention I'm bored?

Maybe I'll give David a call. See what he's up to.

I swear I am so pathetic.

21

"What are you doing here?"

"Hi," I said, peering around him into his living room. "Nice house." And it was—wooden floors, nice thick Oriental rugs, lots of bookcases filled with serious-looking books.

David stood there holding the banana I had obviously interrupted him peeling. "Why are you here?" he repeated.

"I've decided to get back in the game. Really push it academically. I need intense tutoring now. Can I come in?"

I slipped him a twenty as a show of good faith.

He shoved it back in to my hand. "I don't want your money."

"Good. Then you'll just do it as charity. I accept."

My mother had dropped me off, since I can't drive with this leg. I think she was as confused as David was. "Who is this boy?" she wanted to know. She's always approved of Alex. I think she's hoping we'll get back together. We make such a handsome couple.

"Just someone from school," I'd told her.

"Do I know him?" she asked.

"No."

On the ride over I lay across the back seat, leg stretched out, and planned my speech to David: *"You have to help me . . . Hi, whatcha doing? . . . I hope you don't mind . . ."*

Forget it.

David doesn't even understand social norms, so why bother? He does, however, respond to truth, no matter how bizarre.

I went with, "I've been thinking," as I stood there in his doorway. "Do you mind if I come in?"

He held his ground, banana still half-peeled. "You've been thinking what?"

"I didn't really explain what I meant the other day—about dying and everything. I thought you might want to know more."

"No," he said, "I don't."

"Look," I said, shifting on my crutches, "it kind of hurts my armpits to keep standing around like this. Mind if I come in?"

He sighed deeply, but at least he stepped aside and let me come in.

"You can't stay," he said. "I'll give you a ride home."

"Are you this rude to everyone?"

"Cara, this is my house. I didn't invite you. Why are you here?"

"Mind if I sit down?" I asked.

"Fine. But only for a minute." He led me into the kitchen.

I got as comfortable as I could on one of the hard-backed chairs at their kitchen table. I knew David wouldn't know you're supposed to ask someone if they want something to drink, so I helped him out. "Can I have a glass of water?"

He didn't answer, just got me one.

Then he sat across from me.

"First of all," I said, "I really do need your help with calc. It's crazy how far behind I am just from missing that week. And from slacking a little too much this week. I really will pay you—"

"What is it with you and money?" he asked. "I told you I don't want it."

"Fine." There he was making me nervous again. Why can't I ever say what he wants to hear? Or why can't he take a turn and say the right thing to me for once? "It's just that I feel funny about asking you to do it for free."

David stared at me, expressionless.

I took a breath and pushed on. "Okay, second, I know it was rude to come over without calling first—"

"Or being invited. Or being told affirmatively not to come."

"Right." I couldn't handle his eyes, so I concentrated on the blue and white checked placemat in front of me. "It's just that I couldn't hang out at my house another minute. I've been so bored it's driving me crazy, and I thought maybe if you weren't doing anything today . . ."

"So you had someone drop you off without knowing whether I'd be home."

"Right." I kept my gaze on the placemat. It had a nice blue fringe.

"Is this more of your campaign to make friends with me?" David asked. I glanced up to see if he was joking, and his face told me he wasn't. So I knew I had to give him a straight answer.

"Yes. And this is the kind of things friends do on a Saturday morning. We hang out."

David glanced at the clock. "We don't hang out much longer. Ready to go?"

I heard a door open, and David cursed.

Which certainly fed my curiosity.

"Davey?" called a woman's voice.

David stood. "Let's go."

I took my time getting up. I wasn't about to let him rush me out of there. I had the feeling I was about to learn a little bit more about the mysterious Mr. Mayer.

His parents walked into the kitchen. His mother was nice-looking—small, with short brown hair streaked with gray. She wore hiking pants, a fleece sweater, and hiking boots. Dr. Mayer wore something similar. His hair was thinner than David's, but just as messy.

Mrs. Mayer smiled at me. "Hello." She waited a second, then added, "Davey, aren't you going to introduce us?"

David rolled his eyes. He took a step back from the table, held his hands palm upward as if he were serving me on a platter, and announced, "Cara Campbell, NDE."

His mother lost her smile. Whereas the father found his.

Mrs. Mayer stared at me with that same open-mouthed expression David had given me right before he drove off the other day.

She advanced. "Cara—Campbell, did you say?" She shook my hand hard. "Is that true?"

"Yeah," I answered, wondering what all the drama was about. "Campbell. My father owns Campbell Motors—"

David cut in. "Well, my parents will be studying you now. Goodbye." He turned and stalked of the kitchen.

Mrs. Mayer was still holding on to my hand. Gradually she had increased the pressure.

"I hope you have some time." She nodded to her husband, who left the kitchen, too.

"Time for what?"

"Davey must have told you," she said.

I was sick of all the mystery. Apparently no one in that household knew how to give it straight. "What are you talking about?"

Dr. Mayer returned, carrying a handheld digital movie camera and a yellow legal notepad. He handed the paper to his wife and she got up to get a pen.

"Would one of you please tell me what's going on?" For all I knew, they made porn movies with young women David lured to the house.

"We're researching," Mrs. Mayer explained. "For a book we're writing together. I'm surprised Davey didn't tell you."

"Well," I said making no effort to hide my irritation, "he didn't."

"We're writing a book about the soul," she said. "And reincarnation." She signaled her husband to start filming. "Do you mind if we ask you some questions?"

22

They say there are no coincidences. They say everything happens for a reason, whether it's stepping off a curb and breaking your ankle and then being rescued by a woman who happens to be a nurse and whose brother is the guy you'll end up marrying someday, or it's stalking some geek whose parents are authorities on near-death experiences and the afterlife.

It took me a while to warm up. Because even though they were very nice about it, they were still strangers who were prying into my most personal recent experience, and I wasn't entirely sure how much I should tell them.

They aren't wackos. I had to make sure of that before I told them anything. Mrs. Mayer took the time to explain how they came to be interested in the whole topic, and why it was that Dr. Mayer decided to take a leave of absence and do all the medical and clinical research while Mrs. Mayer handled the research side.

"Davey must have told you about Jilly," Mrs. Mayer said.

"No," I said. "David hasn't really told me anything."

"Oh." Mrs. Mayer glanced at her husband. "Well, our daughter—Davey's little sister Jilly—died a few years ago."

I wasn't expecting that—David had certainly never hinted at any family tragedy. But then what has ever told me about himself except that he can beat cashiers at adding?

"I'm so sorry," I said. "How . . . old was she?"

"Only nine," Mrs. Mayer said. Her husband kept filming and said nothing. Easy to see where David gets his communication skills from.

"Car accident," Mrs. Mayer continued. "One of the other mothers was driving the carpool that day . . ." She drifted off, and I saw no reason to make her continue.

"I'm so sorry," I said again. "That's terrible."

"Yes," she agreed. "Anyway." Mrs. Mayer sat up straighter. "Life went on. We thought that was the end of it. Then three years ago Mark had a patient—" She gestured toward her husband. "You tell her."

Dr. Mayer turned off the camera and laid it on the table. "Thirty-five-year-old female," he said. "We'll call her Janine. She came to me for help with anxiety. I worked with her for several months, but nothing seemed to help—her insomnia grew worse, her panic attacks grew more frequent—so at lunch with one of my colleagues I brought up her case and asked for any suggestions he might have. He told me he'd had success with hypnosis. I've tried that a few times over the years, but always found talk therapy to be a much better method. But Janine's symptoms, as I said, were getting worse, and I wanted to try alternative therapies before simply prescribing more medications—she'd already been on several and not responded well.

"It was in our fourth hypnosis session—so far they'd been uneventful—but suddenly her posture changed and she began speaking to me in a voice much deeper and . . . entirely different from her own."

Mrs. Mayer broke in. "She told him about Jilly. She knew everything about her—what she was wearing the day of the accident, where she was sitting in the car, what the other driver did, how Jilly . . . died—"

"She told me things no one had any reason to know," Dr. Mayer resumed. "She knew Jilly's favorite stuffed animal, what songs she loved to sing—"

"What she had said to me that morning before she left for school—" Mrs. Mayer's voice hitched. She paused to clear her throat. "It was remarkable."

"What do you think happened?" I asked them both. "I mean, how did your patient know all that?"

"I believe she was channeling knowledge from some

other source," Dr. Mayer said. "Janine had no way of accessing any of that information herself. I believe some other . . . entity spoke through her."

That gave me goosebumps. I rubbed my arms.

Mrs. Mayer smiled. "I know. I get that way, too."

"So what happened?" I asked. "What else did she say?"

"This . . . entity," Dr. Mayer said, "came to me in three more sessions. He or she—I don't know which—was . . . in contact with Jilly." Now it was Dr. Mayer's turn to clear his throat. "She . . . wanted to tell me—tell us," he said, looking at his wife, "that she was all right. That she was happy. And that she'd always known this was going to be a short life. She told us . . . not to be sad."

Dr. Mayer looked out the window and cleared his throat again.

I couldn't believe they were telling me all this. It was all so personal. And so . . . weird.

"So," Mrs. Mayer said softly, "here we are. We decided this was a much more important pursuit than Mark's regular practice or my life as a litigator." She smiled. "Trust me, it was a little hard for our colleagues to understand why we'd leave everything to give ourselves over to this project."

"Hard for Davey, too," Dr. Mayer added. "He has a hard time . . ."

"Believing," Mrs. Mayer finished.

Oh. Right. Suddenly that moment made sense—that moment when I was standing outside David's car and confessed I'd died. If he wasn't into his parents' project, no wonder he peeled out of there. I was just one more (this is weird to think about, but) freak in his life. Another woo-woo beyond-the-grave weirdo.

It made me smile. David thought *I* was the freak.

"What's funny?" Mrs. Mayer asked, returning my smile.

"It's just that . . . well, David didn't react so well when he found out about me."

Dr. Mayer turned the camera on again. "And now it's your turn to tell us about that."

23

I told them everything—everything I could remember, at least. That included things I didn't even know I remembered.

Dr. Mayer corrected me about one thing right away: what I had wasn't a case of reincarnation, but resurrection, which is apparently a totally separate deal. Resurrection is dying and coming back to life in your own body ("Like Jesus and Lazarus," Mrs. Mayer said, which felt a little odd to be compared to). Reincarnation, on the other hand, is about dying and coming back in a new body and a new life.

It's exactly what the woman in the gray space was trying to tell me about why I couldn't win a new body—not that I wanted one—in what Dr. Mayer decided to call "Life Poker." They'd never heard of that before—I guess

I'm the first person they've talked to who's brought it up. That's kind of cool. And I like the name—it's a lot easier than calling it the card game with the blobs of light.

We talked for three hours. And even though I was starving and sore from sitting so long, I think I could have talked to them for another five days if they had asked me to.

David only drifted in a couple of times, once to grab a container of pasta out of the fridge and eat it cold while leaning against the sink. I could smell the garlic.

"I didn't ask her here," he told his parents. "You do realize that, right?"

"There are no coincidences," his mother answered. "Right, Cara?"

I nodded, feeling strangely smug toward David. His parents and I knew things he didn't. He was purposely keeping himself from knowing as much as we did. Very odd.

Mrs. Mayer kept talking about God. At one point I felt it necessary to tell her my family only goes to church a few times a year—I didn't want her to get the wrong idea about me. I told her I believe in God, but I'm not particularly religious.

"Religion and spirituality are different things," Mrs. Mayer said. "I don't consider myself religious, either. But I definitely believe we have souls. And I believe there are 'entities,' as Mark calls them, all around us."

"Like what?" I asked.

David was there for that. I saw him roll his eyes as his mother answered me.

"Angels, spirit guides—"

"Faeries," David said. "Wood nymphs—"

Mrs. Mayer didn't seem to mind—or notice—his tone. "Who knows?" she told him. "The Kingdom of God is greater than any of us can guess."

"Well, I'll be off to study reality now," David said. "Remember that?"

"Good," Mrs. Mayer said. "You know what Maimonides said about God preferring the prepared mind."

"Here we go," David said, rolling his eyes again.

That made me curious. "Who's—"

"Maimonides," Mrs. Mayer said. "An ancient Jewish scholar. He said that to attain the love of God, we should know math and science, since it provides us with knowledge of God's works, and therefore brings us closer to God."

David grumbled something and promptly left.

Mrs. Mayer smiled and leaned forward conspiratorially. "He hates it when I say things like that."

I couldn't believe David was so cold to his parents—especially considering how nice they are. But I guess it shouldn't surprise me—it is David, after all. Doctor Charm.

"Davey doesn't approve," Mrs. Mayer said. "You probably noticed that."

"Yeah."

"I think it's been hard for him," she said. "Moving away from Denver, transferring to a new school."

"Why did you move?" I asked.

"We felt it would be better for all of us—and for our work—if we got out of the city," she answered. "And I think it has helped—although Davey would still disagree."

I thought about the life David has here now. I almost asked whether he had friends at his old school, but thought that might be giving too much away. David probably hasn't told his parents what life is like at Pinedale High.

And I couldn't help but feel guilty for my part in that.

So I went with a different nosy question. "Did David have a girlfriend back in Denver?"

"Not really," his mother answered. "He was still pretty young."

"Oh. Sure."

David's mother and I both studied each other for a moment. I broke first. "Does he have one . . . now?"

Mrs. Mayer smiled. "We thought maybe you would know best."

Great. Did they think I was his girlfriend?

"Um, David and I don't really . . ."

Dr. Mayer saved me. "Davey keeps to himself. He always has."

"Yes," I said. "He does." And even though it probably wasn't cool to involve them, I added, "But I would like to get to know him better, you know? I've been trying, but . . ."

Mrs. Mayer smiled. "You're very kind for trying."

Ugh. No, I wasn't. If only they knew. I was probably one of the reasons why their son's last two years in Pinedale haven't been fun at all. And now the only reason I'm trying to change that is because of my own bizarre experience with resurrection.

I had left that part out of my story—the part where I saw their son's face. So sue me. They don't need to know everything.

But obviously I'm getting closer to my answer. Because so far the trail has led directly from David to the two people—maybe the only two people—in my town who know anything at all about what I went through.

Like Mrs. Mayer said—there are no coincidences.

24

O h, my God. This is fascinating.

Before I left, David's parents gave me a copy of the manuscript they're working on. It's called *The Soul in Transit*. It's full of the most incredible stories.

One is about this brother and sister who were in their forties, but still fought like they did when they were kids. Literally—punching, kicking, screaming, throwing food—the works.

So they go into therapy, and the sister agrees to try hypnosis to see if she can discover what it is in their childhoods that makes them hate each other so.

Well, it wasn't their childhoods at all. It was a love affair back in the 1800s. She was single, he was married, and he got her pregnant. He promised to marry her. When the day of their wedding came, the groom was nowhere to be found. Turns out he had left with his wife for a sort of second honeymoon the day before. The pregnant woman had to find out from the guy's servant. So she goes back to her shabby rooms, climbs up to the roof, and throws herself off.

A pretty good reason to hold a grudge.

But there's more. The brother goes in for his own hypnosis session, and his story is completely different. His story is about the two of them being soldiers together in some war in the 12th century, and his sister (who was a man in that life, obviously) abandoned him during battle and let him slowly bleed to death from a hideous leg wound. Jeez. So he'd been holding that against her for only 900 years. No problem.

And then they both remembered this one life from the 1920s, when she was his mother. She was a drunk and a prostitute, and she left him alone while she went out to turn tricks, and one night he wandered onto the fire escape and lost his footing and plunged to his death.

What a happy family.

But somehow airing all those old grievances really did the trick. Brother and sister could finally forgive and love each other in this lifetime. Happily ever after. Or at least until the next lifetime when one of them screws up.

The Mayers' book says that people tend to reincarnate in clusters. That means families stick together, working out their issues one lifetime after another. It doesn't say when or if the cycle ever gets to stop. Maybe you're constantly making it up to your relatives for all of eternity.

It makes me appreciate the relationship I have with Beth. I can't imagine how things would be if we were both resenting some crime against each other from way back when. It's interesting, though, to think about who Beth might have been to me before. Has she always been my sister? Or maybe my mother some of the time? Or maybe even my husband?

No, that's too weird.

It makes me feel good to know the same people keep wanting to hang around with me life after life. Who needs people like Toomy when I have my own cluster of reincarnated souls right here in my own house?

I was sort of skipping ahead in the book, even though I plan to go back and read it all. But I really wanted to see what they had to say about resurrection.

The stories were pretty much like mine: a brief death, some out-of-body experience, then return to the body and go on from there.

But the people are always transformed.

They see their lives in a different way afterward—a more purposeful way. They go back to college, or marry that guy they were afraid to commit to before. They have children when they didn't think they wanted to before. They start companies that manufacture products that improve the lives of millions. They are, in short, spectacular.

And I am still just me.

One woman talked about how she died while giving birth to her second child. She had this whole review-your-life kind of experience, and saw her many, many failings. When she woke up, she thought she really had died because her father was there dressed in a dark suit. Turns out he had rushed to the hospital from a business meeting. But she thought he was dressed for her funeral. So for a good ten minutes she kept right on believing she had really died, no matter what people were trying to tell her.

She said it was the most profound, horrifying, invigorating experience of her life. To really see what it was like to die—feel the feelings, watch her life flash before her, and move on to her own funeral even though it wasn't. She came out of that experience feeling amazingly calm about everything. About waiting in line for things, about being put on hold, about her kids screaming, her husband's snoring, her weight, her mother's nagging about her weight, the state of the world, the rise in crime—everything.

Because she got it. And this is what I'm trying to pay attention to, because I want to get it, too.

It's kind of like my theory about Time. The woman who thought she died says that now she understands how gentle life is. She is no longer afraid of death. She is no longer afraid of pain. Every bad thing that can happen to us during our lives only lasts a second, then it's gone. It's our own messed up minds that keep going over and over things, making ourselves miserable. If you just let go, lie back and let the flow of life carry you along, all is well, all is peaceful, all is bliss.

All is bliss.

I'm going to try that. I'm going to try just closing my eyes and letting life be however it wants to be. I'm going to try not worrying about anything—including whether I'm doing what I'm supposed to do with my life.

Try it. See.

I think I'm getting better at all this.

25

Alex will not give up. I hope he's my brother in some future life so I can hit him over the head with a frying pan.

Believe it or not, another wee-hours visit. Guess his date with Kimberly didn't get him what he wanted, because there he was beneath my window around three this morning, tossing pebbles as well as he could in his highly drunken state. Shows what all that cross-training during baseball season can do for a guy.

What a pig. Again I have to ask myself, how could I? I gave my virginity to that guy. I honestly had feelings of love for that guy. I thought I was so lucky to have such a great-looking boyfriend. I thought I had really hit the peak of what I could get at Pinedale High.

Close your eyes. Relax. Let the flow take you.

Okay, so that's what I tried to do. I calmly accepted the fact that my drunken ex-boyfriend was downstairs trying to get me to let him in so he could stick it somewhere I wasn't going to let him stick.

So I descended the stairs calmly. Calmly I opened the door and felt the blast of cold night air and the fumes from Alex's mouth.

He tried hard to stand up straight as he asked me, "What the f—, Cara? What's your deal?"

I resisted the urge to slam the door. I said calmly, "Alex, you have to understand. I don't want to go out with you anymore. I honestly wish you well in whatever you do. But you cannot come to my house anymore, whether it's during the day or at night. Do you understand me?"

He swayed and gripped the door frame for balance. "Why you being such a f—ing—"

"No," I corrected him, "I am not being a f—ing anything. Please get that through your head. And since I know that's what you care about most—"

And then he tried to look all sorrowful. "C'mon, babe, I miss you!"

"Shhh. You'll wake up my parents."

He reached for me and I pulled back. I'm actually getting pretty good on my crutches.

"Don't you love me anymore?" he wailed.

And I couldn't help it. I laughed.

"Bitch!"

"Shhh!"

I heard the top stair squeak. Someone was up there listening.

Which I was grateful for, just in case.

I tried one more time. "I did love you, Alex, but I realize now I was too immature for that kind of relationship. I respect you," I lied, even though the words made me want to VOMIT, "but I don't want a relationship with you anymore. I know we'll both be happier this way."

I turned toward the stairs and took a guess. "It's okay, Mom, I'll be right up. Alex just wanted to say goodbye."

I turned back to him. "Goodbye, Alex. I appreciate everything you were to me. We have to move on."

And then I took a chance and started swinging the door closed. But Alex didn't try to stop me. He just stood there looking stupid and drunk, gazing into my face longingly as if I were leaving on the Titanic in the morning.

I flipped the dead-bolt. And sagged against the wall.

Beth took two more steps down until I could see her in the light.

"You are my hero," she said.

I was shaking, but not as badly as the last time.

"Please date only ugly boys," I told my sister. "They're so much easier to handle."

"Is that why you're going out with David?"

"No. He's not that ugly and we're not going out."

"Ha. So you admit it—you think he's cute."

"No, I don't admit it."

"He's kind of like a mutt," Beth said. "You know? All scruffy and everything, but he has this cute lovable face and you know you just have to bring him home."

Unreal. It was past three in the morning, I'd just given my drunken ex-boyfriend the heave ho—again—and here was my little sister talking about how David reminds her of a dog.

"Beth, it's late—"

"I'm just saying," she persisted. "I think he's really cute."

"So what are you telling me, that you have some crush on David Mayer? You've only met him twice."

"Yeah, but he kind of sticks with you, don't you think?"

Oh, my God. It's not enough that I have visions of David Mayer as I'm resurrected, now I have to deal with my little sister having a thing for him.

Relax. Go with the flow.

"Beth, you're way too young to start thinking about this. Come back to me in a year. Or two—two is better."

"He might be taken by then."

"Oh, I'm pretty sure not."

I'm back. Super-Anal Straight-A Girl is back. I feel SO much better.

I've been thinking about what David's mother said—about how knowing math and science is a way to understand God. Or however she put it.

Maybe that's exactly the kind of sign I've been looking for. Maybe I had it exactly backwards: I'm not supposed to drop science and math, I'm supposed to kick their ASS.

Same for history and English and Spanish. I'm supposed to be smart. I drew the smart card—I know that's true. It feels too wrong and miserable to be a slacker. God must want me to be brilliant.

I've been thinking a lot about God. How could I not? I read some more of the Mayers' book yesterday, and it's filled with atheists and agnostics seeing the light. Literally—lots of Near Death Experiences (NDEs, as I will now call them, because I am part of that club)—lots of them die and see some sort of light, and sometimes even a bodiless ball of light like mine, and they feel guided and safe, and they believe that figure is God.

I don't think I saw God. I think I saw people just like me, at different stages of their lives. They were choosing new lifetimes, and I was going back to mine, but we were all just humans trying to get it right.

If God was there, he was hiding, watching. I don't think I'm sorry I didn't see him. I think that would have seriously messed me up.

One of the huge benefits of walking around today contemplating God and the afterlife and all things other-worldly is that I could not care even the slightest what crude little remarks and glares my former friends threw me. They'll get over me soon—I know that. I'm not bothering them, and soon they'll forget about me. What a relief that will be.

David was pretty weird to me in class and at lunch. Like he's ashamed around me all of a sudden. Like I've exposed some big dark secret of his, and now I'm going to say or do something to humiliate him.

Which, to be fair, the old me might have done just for kicks. Not proud of it, but I'm not going to lie about it, either.

I sat across from him again at lunch, and this

time he really ignored me—wouldn't even look up from his book, even when I reached over and tapped the pages. He just got up, threw out the rest of his lunch (bagel with garlic cream cheese—good God, that guy needs a clue), and left me there all by myself.

Fine. I had lots of homework to catch up on. It felt good to be back in the groove, pushing myself mentally. If I can't push my body, at least I can overwork my head.

I couldn't help glancing over at the jocks' table, and sure enough, Alex was staring at me and saying something to Toomy, who was also staring at me. Didn't care. At all.

I like this whole calm thing. It's really working. Nothing can bother me if I don't let it.

Wonder what's up with David?

I'm tempted to stick a note under the windshield wiper on his car. QUIT WITH THE GARLIC. GIRLS WILL LIKE YOU BETTER.

Hey, maybe Beth is on to something—bring home the mutt and clean him up and brush out his fur.

Maybe that's one of my tasks during this lifetime— to transform David Mayer into some sort of sex god.

No, not.

What is his problem, though? I'm a nice girl, aren't I? At least I am this time. And it's not like I'm trying to date him—I just want to be able to sit across from him at the losers' lunch table without getting snubbed. Is that so much to ask?

His was the face I saw when I woke up. He, David Mayer, has to mean something.

Not easy being an NDE. Good thing I'm seeing a psychiatrist this weekend.

The Mayers want me back.

At least some of them.

27

After school I followed David to his car. My mom was picking me up, so I didn't have much time, but what is Time to the afterdead?

"You don't like your parents' work," I said.

"How perceptive of you." He pulled out his keys and prepared to blow me off.

"Why?"

"I don't remember deciding my life was your business."

I grabbed his arm. "What's your hurry? Come on. Talk to me."

He turned and gave me his most superior look. "Still looking for help with calc?"

"No, I'm back on and you know it." He'd been there in class this morning—he'd seen.

David shook his head. "Still looking for a new friend?"

"Come on, David, cut the crap."

"What crap?" he said angrily. "You impose yourself on me, my family—"

"Your parents seem to like me. Unlike you."

"My parents are fantasists."

"Fanta—"

"I am a realist. You want to talk to me on my terms, fine. But now that you're their new pet project—"

"Is that it?" I said. "You're jealous?"

David smiled, but not in a friendly way. "Look, I don't know why you picked me out—"

"I told you. I had a vision of you or something."

"Good. And I'm sure somewhere out there someone is having visions of you—"

"This isn't personal," I said. "I'm not trying to date you." I added, more to myself than him, "I wish you were gay. Then we wouldn't have this problem."

Now he was angry. "Do you even think about things before they come out of your mouth?"

He got into his car and slammed the door before I could pin my body in there. Which is probably good, since I doubt in his frame of mind he would have watched out for my leg.

I wasn't ready to give up. "I just think since I'm going to be spending some time at your house—"

"Don't worry," David said, "I won't disturb you."

"What is your problem?" I asked. "I told you I wanted to be friends and I do."

"Well, I don't." He turned the key in the ignition, and this time I had the sense to take a step back before he pulled away.

He almost hit my mom as they passed. She honked. Good.

I threw my backpack into the back and added my leg to the pile. The rest of me climbed in after.

"Everything okay?" my mother asked.

"I'm sick of this thing," I said, pointing to my ungainly leg.

"Honey, I'm sure it's frustrating—"

"You don't even know," I said. "I can already feel how much weight I've gained. My whole body is a big squishy fat globule."

My mother smiled consolingly. "Cara, you know that's not true. You've barely been eating."

I punched the back of the seat. It felt good. "I need to work out."

"Doctor Hastings doesn't want you to reinjure your leg."

"I don't care. I hate just sitting around."

"Please," my mother said, "wait just a little longer. We want you to be healthy."

She faced forward again and started driving toward home. I stared out the window and fumed.

Who is David Mayer to pull any kind of attitude

with me? I have been nothing but polite to that guy. I don't see anyone else making the trek over to the losers' table and sharing the garlic section with him. He's not a guy who can afford to refuse friends. He's more socially incompetent than I thought.

My mom had to go back to work, of course, so she helped me out of the car but then drove away. Beth wasn't home yet, so it was just me and my lonesome.

I went straight to the laundry room and pulled out what I needed.

My body will not be denied.

2 8

I saw this old movie on TV a few years ago called *Heaven Can Wait*. It's about a football player who dies while biking through a tunnel, and when he gets up to heaven he finds out they made a mistake—he was actually supposed to survive, but his guardian angel or whatever it was saw what was going down and decided to pull him out of his body and let him avoid all that pain. Big mistake. By the time it all gets sorted out, the guy's body has already been cremated, so that's no longer an option. Instead they find another body for him—some fat rich guy who's just been knocked off by his wife and her lover.

And the thing that I loved most—not realizing that one day I would die, too, and I would feel the exact same way—is that the reincarnated guy accepts that this new body isn't perfect—it's way too fat and slow—but he figures he can change all that.

So he starts working out like crazy, and soon enough the new body isn't looking so bad. It can even do what his old body could.

That's me. I happen to be back in my original body, but it's not the way it's supposed to be. Maybe my mother's right and I haven't technically gained any weight—in fact, I may technically be down a few pounds—but it's not the pounds, it's the feeling. I feel soft. I feel weak. I feel like I'm not in my right body.

I worked out last night for the first time in weeks. WAY too long for me.

I carried all my free weights upstairs from the laundry room, one at a time (not so easy on crutches and on stairs), and now they're safely stowed under my bed where I can work out with them any time.

Which, last night, meant about every five minutes.

I don't want my mom to know. She'll worry that I'm going to push myself too hard and reinjure the leg. Fat chance. I never want this leg to be weak again. I will baby it, but I will also require things of it. It must start to bend. Not much, but at least a little. I tried it last night, and boy it hurt, but it was a good hurt. Like I'd rediscovered a lost limb.

I can do a lot in my present condition. Push-ups against the wall, balanced on my good leg. Sit-ups. Biceps, triceps, lats, delts—the whole range of arm and back exercises. Leg lifts, although I have to wear the brace for that, which means one leg is heavier than the other one, but I can adapt. The point is, I'm moving again. I'm not just sitting around waiting for my body to come to me—I'm going to it.

Slight change in plans: suspend—no, probably retire —this whole encyclopedia plan. I was flipping through it yesterday and came to *Fennec, a small fox living in the deserts of North Africa,* and it occurred to me I was never *ever* going to use that information in my life. But my leg? Think I'll be using that. So library time is now rehab time. Do some leg extensions, brace off. I figure if I can increase my range of motion even a fraction of a millimeter each day, in time I will have my leg back to where it was.

The whole body needs to hum again. I may not be able to run for a while, or ski, or play soccer or softball or any of it, but I can build my muscles again, top to bottom (literally—my butt feels like a pillow), and one day in the glorious future I will be Me again.

Me Improved, I should say. Me the Sequel—bigger, stronger, better.

I'm over David Mayer. I've tried hard enough to be that guy's friend. I realize now that the only reason I must have seen that vision or whatever of him was to lead me to his parents. I don't know who put that vision in my head—whether it was God or that woman or even me, my soul—but I know enough now to pay attention to things like that. There are no coin-cidences.

So here's where we stand, on this Tuesday afternoon as I sit outside on one of the benches near the admin building, soaking in some sun while everyone else in my class is inside having lunch:

Friends: 0

Souls: 1

Bodies: 1

Hope: Much

Plans: Many

Days until Dr. Mayer hypnotizes me and I find out more about my NDE: 4

Seconds I was dead: 42

Years I wasted: 16

Years I want to live a better life: Forever

29

It's Friday. I've been working out like a fiend. Writing secret codes on my calendar, keeping track of number of reps, size of weight, what I'm eating—all of it. I am my own project. I am that guy in *Heaven Can Wait* looking at his whole body situation thinking, *"What can I do to rebuild this?"*

One thing I can do is eat. I've been pounding back the milk, yogurt, beans, spinach, oatmeal, fruit, salads. I know my muscles would be thrilled to get some meat in there, but I can't bring myself to eat it. I don't know if I ever will be able to again. For now, we'll have to get by on eggs (which I don't mind) and tofu (ditto).

I am back on top in my classes. Other than calc, where Mayer totally kicks my butt, I am clearly the winner in preparation, quiz-taking, and—face it—style.

I've stopped dressing like the homeless. I'm back to my Adidas pants and my favorite lycra tops, and except for the bulky brace around my knee, my profile is looking normal again.

But I swear my arms are bigger. Even though it's only been a few days, I can feel every muscle as I build it. I think this might be the perfect opportunity to balance out my monster quads with some equally-monster arms and shoulders. What can it hurt? Besides, I'm curious to see just what this body can do if I give it as much attention as I have been all week.

I'm ready for Dr. Mayer. I finished their book last night. I ended up re-reading a bunch of sections, just to make sure I understand.

Like this concept of xenoglossy. Some people who are revisiting their past lives while under hypnosis actually start talking in a foreign language—even though it's one they never learned in this lifetime. One woman was born and raised in a small town in Texas, and suddenly under hypnosis she was talking in fluent French. The hypnotist had a tape recorder going, and afterward he got one of the professors at a nearby college to translate it. Turns out the woman had lived in France during the Crusades. Her husband went off to convert heathens, and she missed him so much she died of a broken heart. Apparently that can really happen.

Another guy—some big white trucker whose wife

dragged him to a weekend hypnosis seminar—started speaking Swahili. Some woman in the audience recognized the dialect—turns out the trucker had lived in her old village in a previous life.

But my favorite story—not about xenoglossy, but about past lives—is the one about the man and woman who didn't know each other, but both ended up going to the same therapist for help quitting smoking. One week the therapist hypnotized the man so he could implant messages about smoking being bad for him (duh), and during the session the patient started recalling some past life in Munich, Germany when he was a doctor in the first world war.

Then the woman comes in the following week—and remember, these people don't know each other—and she's hypnotized, learning that smoking is bad for her (duh), and suddenly she starts telling the exact same story about living in Munich during the war and falling in love with this doctor and blah, blah, blah, unhappily ever after.

So the therapist is going nuts, right? Because he can't divulge patient confidentiality by saying, "Oh, and I happen to know your former husband." So week after week he keeps seeing these people, all the while wishing they would just find each other and get back together again.

Well, of course Fate intervenes, because that is what Fate is for. The woman has to reschedule her appointment, and then the man does, too, and miraculously they both end up with sessions back to back on the same day. The man is just leaving as the woman is just coming. And their eyes meet, and . . .

Nothing.

At least not at first.

The woman overhears the man talking to the receptionist about his next appointment, and she learns that his last name is Denumpleck, which is obviously not a common name. She says, "Oh, I went to school with a girl named Allison Denumpleck," and he says, "Really? That's my sister." And they get to talking, and the therapist comes out to summon the woman in to her appointment, and he nearly bursts into tears to see the two of them finally talking.

Gotta love that.

Of course they end up dating, of course they end up married, and as far as anyone knows, it's a lovely relationship. Whatever sorrow they shared in their previous life, it appears to be healed in this one.

God. I love that.

I don't know if Dr. Mayer is going to ask me about any past lives, or if he's going to stick to what happened in the gray space.

Maybe if we have time I'll ask him to do both. I wonder if I'll speak Swahili.

30

My mom dropped me off about 10:00 this morning (thinking I was studying with my new math friend, David—okay, so I lied). Dr. and Mrs. Mayer had gone on a coffee run. David let me in, then disappeared back into his hole. I sat in the living room and waited.

"Do your parents know you're doing this?" Mrs. Mayer asked me when they came back.

"Oh. Sure," I lied. Again. I can't believe I can't even stick to one resolution. But it happens to be the hardest one.

"Good," Mrs. Mayer said. "Because even though we're doing research, and Mark isn't technically treating you as a patient, I'd be more comfortable if your parents signed a release for you. Can I send you home with one?"

"Sure." The new me is going to have to learn how to forge her parents' signatures.

Yes, dishonest, and yes, I'm trying to do better, but there's no point in alarming my parents, and even less point in doing anything to interfere with the Mayers helping me. I'm sure the woman in the gray space would understand.

The three of us went back into their home office. It was a lot messier in there than the rest of the house—big overflowing bookshelves, a desk buried under stacks of paper—but it had this huge, comfortable leather couch. I stretched out and they gave me a blanket for my legs and a little beanbag strip to lay over my eyes to block the light out.

This time Mrs. Mayer did the filming, while Dr. Mayer hypnotized me.

I didn't think it was working at first.

I was relaxed, but not in trance or anything. I could tell what was going on around me. Dr. Mayer's voice was very soothing, but there was nothing special about what he was saying or how he was saying it. Just various quiet commands, like "Count backward from 100," and "picture a stream," and "lift your arm," and before I knew it, bingo.

"Describe the woman," Dr. Mayer said, and so I looked at her really carefully. The thick brown hair.

The soft, loving eyes. The easy smile. Her body. That tunic-like thing she was wearing. The things she was saying.

And here's what's really interesting: I had forgotten some of what she actually said. All this time I've had a general impression of what she told me, but I had been missing the actual words.

What she said was this: "You have taken the wrong path."

That's all.

Not, "You've been wasting your life," or "you shouldn't do sports," or "you need to completely change everything about yourself."

She did ask me the question I remembered before—that part about what I wanted to change. But she was just asking, not telling me. She never said I had to change anything. Just that I had taken the wrong path.

What does that mean?

And when? At what point did I take it?

Did I start going the wrong way when I was little, or just the week before my operation? If I had half a brain I would have asked her for more specifics.

Think about it logically: would a God or some supreme being have ripped me from my body and brought me up to the gray space for counseling if I'd only made a little mistake? No. So it had to be huge. Which is why, I guess, I came away with the impression that I'd made some monumental misstep—like thinking

I was Athlete, and not Brain Surgeon or something else more important. But the woman's actual words don't really tell me much at all.

Not what I wanted to hear.

I thought I'd come out of today's session feeling perfectly at peace and enlightened. I thought I'd finally solve that one missing piece of the puzzle—what it is exactly I'm supposed to be doing with my life.

Dr. Mayer could see my disappointment. "Not what you expected?"

I cleared my throat and shook my head. I almost wanted to cry.

Mrs. Mayer came over to sit beside me on the couch. She put her arm around me. "Let's take a little break. Then do you want to try again?"

I did. And that's what led me to the truth.

31

———

It was 1933. I was pregnant and poor. We lived on a farm in Oklahoma.

My husband was Alex.

I recognized him right away. He was in a different body, of course, and his name was Charles, but it didn't matter. I knew him the same way I knew myself—that poor pregnant woman with the bruises on her throat.

I flinched whenever he came near. He talked to me like I was a dog. I was feeling sick—it was early in the pregnancy—and it slowed me down, and that made him madder. I wasn't cooking right, cleaning right, giving him enough sex.

I hated the sex.

He was rough with me. Just jammed it in without trying in the slightest way to warm me up. He wouldn't kiss me—barely even looked at me while he was doing it. I just turned my head and held my breath until it was over.

His mother lived with us, and she was a wretched woman. She's not someone I recognized. She was old and gnarled and had nothing but insults for me—how I was stupid and ugly and a low-class cow who had tricked her son into marrying me.

Some trick.

I wanted to reach into that memory and physically pull myself out. Take me away somewhere safe and warm. Slap the old woman across the mouth. Take Alex's head and ram it against the wall.

I could hear Dr. Mayer's questions the whole time, in some remote part of my brain: "Let yourself watch. Let go of any emotion."

I couldn't let go of emotion—it was all I was right then. Not intellectual—not, *"Oh, how interesting, wonder what he'll do next"*—but open, raw emotion: *"Get out! Get out now!"*

I guess I was breathing too fast, because Dr. Mayer decided to bring me out of it before I'd seen everything there was to see. I lay there panting, sweating, sick to my stomach just like the pregnant Louisa had been.

Louisa. That was my name.

I covered my face with my hands. Part of me wanted to go back to the scene, part of me never wanted to see it again.

Mrs. Mayer asked, "Are you all right?"

I nodded, my hands still covering my face.

She handed me a glass of water. All I could think of was how thirsty Louisa was, how tired, how sad, how trapped.

"Want to talk about it?" Dr. Mayer asked me.

I shook my head. "I think I want to go home."

Mrs. Mayer offered to drive me.

As I waited in the living room, hunched over my crutches, still wet from all the sweat, David wandered downstairs and took a look at me.

And actually said something nice.

"You all right?"

"Not really."

"Rough session?"

I nodded.

David leaned against the banister. "You don't have to do this, you know. Just because they're interested—"

His mother came out of the downstairs bathroom. "Ready?"

I exchanged a look with David. He actually seemed concerned.

"Yeah," I said, feeling as weak as I had right after I got home from the surgery. I think all these flights of soul take their toll on me. Maybe we're not meant to spend so much time out of our bodies.

"See ya," I told David.

"See ya," he said back, and he didn't seem mad at all.

Maybe all I had to do was stand in his living room looking all pasty white, ready to puke, for him to decide I'm an okay person after all.

Mrs. Mayer and I didn't talk much on the ride home. I wished I were already alone.

As I got out she said, "Are you sure you're all right?"

"No, not really."

And I bent in half and puked all over the curb.

32

I haven't told Beth. Because telling Beth might mean telling her more than I want to tell.

I haven't told Beth a lot of things: not about the gray space, not about the Mayers' research or being put under hypnosis.

I have told her about sex. So score one for the older sister.

It's Sunday morning and I still feel like crap. My stomach is still queasy. My head hurts like crazy. I've been lying in bed, unable to muster the strength to get up. I'd love some coffee or tea or something, but apparently my family's powers of telepathy are weak. They have this habit of bothering me when I want to be alone, and abandoning me when I need them. Okay, maybe that's an overstatement, but right now I wish just one of them would bother me.

I don't know what to think. I mean I honestly don't. That whole past-life regression has seriously messed me up. Seeing Alex like that, seeing me like that—that's why I'm still feeling sick. I can't believe how helpless I was.

I want to go back to the Mayers and make them show me a happy story. But what if I don't have any? What if every one of my lives, no matter how many there've been—and Mrs. Mayer says there might have been hundreds—what if every one of them has been just as miserable as that one I saw? I think of myself as a happy person—at least in this life—so there must have been some happiness in my past, right? Unless this is my first shot at it, and here I am already ruining it by obsessing over what I saw.

The sex was DISGUSTING. I mean, I thought I had some bad moments with Alex in this life, but at least he kissed me and bought me little gifts sometimes and pretended he liked me.

God, I feel so sorry for her. Poor Louisa. And those bruises around her neck—they could only have been from his hands, right? Did he try to kill her? Or was it just part of his regular daily abuse?

And what about the mother? Who the hell was she? If I knew she was someone in my life right now, I'd go over to her house and smack her.

Beth just came into my room and I asked her if she'd bring me something warm to drink and she left right away to do it. I love my little sister. Thank God Beth wasn't in that life.

Or maybe she was. Oh, my God, maybe she was the baby inside me. Could that be? Maybe she was the only person I could love and who loved me. No wonder I feel so close to Bethie in this life. She saved me.

Or maybe not. Maybe she died somehow, either in or out of the womb. Maybe Alex beat me and I miscarried. Maybe he beat Beth. Maybe what I'm supposed to do in this life is make it up to her and protect her.

I AM DRIVING MYSELF CRAZY!!!! PEOPLE SHOULD NOT LEARN THESE THINGS ABOUT THEIR PAST LIVES!!!!

What am I supposed to do now? Am I going to be in some psychiatrist's office three hundred years from now—if they still have psychiatrists—and he or she will hypnotize me and I'll look back on this life and get all freaked out and think, "What was she doing? Can't I go back and help her?"

Get a grip.

Beth just came back and she brought me hot chocolate with whipped cream on top. Love her. I asked her to snuggle up on my bed with me for a minute, and she did. She was warm and smelled good, like vanilla lotion. I almost started to tell her, but I couldn't.

If I can't handle it, she certainly can't. I have to

protect her. Who knows what she might remember if I started bringing things up?

I wish I had never met the Mayers. I think I've caused permanent damage.

I'm going to take it easy and rest. Regroup. Then maybe lift weights later if I can drag myself out of this bed.

How many lives have I wasted with Alex?

And how many times have I let him hit me?

I thought once in this lifetime was enough.

33

Monday. My counselor Ms. Josephson called me into her office this morning "to touch base."

"So, how are you feeling?"

"Fine. Much better. I've gotten back to my school work."

"I see that," she said, looking down at some report. "So everything is all right? You're feeling better?"

"Sure. Everything's fine." I started to get up, thinking that was all.

Then she got around to what she really called me in there for. "You seem to have had a falling out with Victoria."

I glanced at the report on her desk. Exactly who was

spying on me and Toomy? "Yeah, well, we don't really have that much in common right now. With me off the team and everything."

"But you're not sitting with her at lunch."

I could feel the red in my face. "It's not really the school's business who my friends are, is it?" I couldn't believe I actually said that, but come on—what was she doing poking her nose into my personal life?

"We like our students to prosper," Ms. Josephson said, "and that includes in their social relationships."

"Look," I said, "Toomy and I—"

And just then the door to Ms. Josephson's office opened, and in walked Coach Toomy.

I stared at him. He smiled. I adjusted my crutches and started to leave.

"Mad at me, too?" he asked.

"I'm not mad at anyone. I just don't play sports anymore, okay? So there's no point in talking to me."

"I'm not just your coach," he said.

I interrupted before he could say, "I'm your friend." Maybe he wasn't going to say that, but it felt like one of those moments.

"I just want to focus on school," I told them both. "There's no point—"

"You didn't have to drop P.E.," he said. "There are other things for you to do while you recover."

Like what? I wanted to ask. *Like hanging around with Alex and Toomy and everyone else, and going right back to my evil ways? I died!* I felt like saying. *And when I came back one of the first things I knew was that I didn't want to be like any of you anymore.*

But of course you don't say things like that. I held my temper. I said politely, "I appreciate the offer, Coach, but I'm going to concentrate on my studies this year."

"This year?" he said. "But my understanding is it's only a few months—"

"I don't want to play sports anymore. I want to do something different."

Coach Toomy looked at me in a way that used to work before. Before, all it took was that stern-eyed, tight-lipped expression, and I'd realize what a failure I'd just been in some event, and vow to push myself harder and harder.

Not this time. He has no hold on me anymore.

"I have to get back to class," I said. "I missed too much school after the operation."

"Your grades are fine," Ms. Josephson said. "There's no rush."

Thanks a lot for the help.

"You should listen to Coach Toomy," she said. "You've been a real asset to this school, Cara, and we'd like to see you get back into the swing of things. What can we do to help?"

God! Is that all people care about? All my sports glories and what they've meant to the school?

"No, thank you," I said with as much control as I could muster. "I quit."

"I thought you were tougher than that," Coach Toomy growled, like that was supposed to cut me.

"Guess not," I said, crutching past him into the hall.

34

At least David was speaking to me again.

I took a chance and sat with him at lunch. He actually looked up from his book.

I took another chance and addressed him about his food. "Um, David, mind if I tell you something?"

He gave me that suspicious look. Can't blame him.

"I want to be your friend," I said. "And friends help each other out."

He just stared and waited.

"So, here's the thing," I said. "I happen to know that girls find you cute." Okay, one girl—my sister—but close enough.

That softened him a little, but he was still wary.

"But you're not really putting yourself in the best

spot, because I have to tell you, you really smell like garlic."

He stared at me with absolutely no expression on his face. "Anything else, Fairy Godmother?"

"Your clothes are a little—"

"Cara, let me explain something." He leaned forward to make sure I was paying attention. "I. Don't. Care. Understand? I don't care what you and your friends think of me—"

"They're not my friends—"

"Or if I smell like garlic or dress wrong or whatever it is you think about me. I don't care what anyone at this school thinks about anything I do. I just want to do my work and get out—the sooner the better. You understand?"

The thing is, I did. I do. I've been feeling that way myself lately.

"What I think you don't understand," he continued, "is that every other word out of your mouth is an insult. You seem to think you're the arbiter of all things cool, and I don't happen to—"

"No, I don't—"

"—agree. I think you're selfish and shallow and—"

"Fine." I held up my hands. "You've made your point." I wished I'd never opened my mouth. I'd never seen him so angry.

"And I don't know what this game is you're playing with my parents."

"Game?" I said. "They asked me, remember? I didn't even know what they did."

"And yet you came over to my house, unannounced, uninvited—"

"Because there are no coincidences," I said. "I was obviously led to them."

David scoffed. "I forgot to say you're also stupid."

Okay, that went too far.

"I am not stupid," I said in a low, tense voice. "I happen to have a 4.0, you *idiot,* and unlike you, I'm not spending every waking hour of my life doing homework and playing math games with myself—"

David just sat there, as bored-looking as always. I wanted to slap him.

"I work out at least two hours every day, I'm on the soccer, ski, *and* softball teams during the year, I've got games or races at least once a week—including away games, which means I have even less time—and that's not including weekend tournaments and playoffs and double practices—and yet somehow I manage to be fourth in our class. Why is that, David? I must be stupid, right? But of course, no one could be as brilliant as you are. Although your parents seem to be awfully smart. And they, unlike you, know how to dress themselves and don't smell like the garbage can outside an Italian restaurant!"

We stared at each other across the table. Then David calmly went back to his book.

"My little sister thought you were nice," I said, not able to stop myself now. "She actually thinks you're cute. She noticed the smell, too," I lied, "but she's been willing to overlook it. You could get girls, you know. Maybe then you'd be a decent human being instead of such a DRIED UP, FRUSTRATED JERK!"

It's hard to storm off when you're on crutches, but I managed pretty well.

Why do I even care? In the beginning I felt some responsibility toward him because I thought maybe he was supposed to mean something to me, but now that I know it's just his parents I was supposed to meet, why even bother trying to fix his life anymore? What a waste of time—and I don't waste Time anymore.

It's just that he's the densest, most socially retarded person I've ever met, and if he'd just listen to me—

This is not how I want to spend my life. Three hundred years from now I'll be looking back on today thinking, *"Move on! Go do something important with your-self! Why are you talking to him?"*

I need to talk to my psychiatrist. I really think I'm losing my mind.

35

In *The Soul in Transit,* there's a section about the reasons for resurrection.

That ancient scholar Mrs. Mayer mentioned before —Maimonides—said that resurrection allows a soul another opportunity to mature and attain a higher level of relationship to God.

Maybe that's what I'm missing. Maybe I was supposed to come down from the gray space and immediately embrace my religion and find God with my new mature soul.

The book goes on to talk about all the resurrection stories in the Bible. In the Old Testament, there's Ezekiel's vision of going to the Valley of Dry Bones. God breathes the breath of life into the bones, and immediately sinews start to grow, knitting the bones back together. Then the organs, the skin, and soon the bones are all living, breathing humans.

Then there's the story of King Saul and the ghost of the prophet Samuel. Things aren't going well for King Saul, so he visits the Witch of Endor and asks her to summon up the spirit of Samuel. Samuel is very annoyed by this—basically, "Why are you disturbing my rest?"—and then he tells King Saul that the very next day Saul and his sons will die in battle. Proving you don't want to wake the dead. Samuel is a ghost, not a resurrected body, but he still proves that in ancient biblical times the soul could come and go.

The real spate of resurrections happens during Jesus's time. He raised at least four or five people, including himself and Lazarus. Lazarus was in the tomb four days before Jesus called to him to come out. Lazarus stepped out, still wearing the strips of linen they'd used to embalm him. He was the first walking mummy.

Do you think Lazarus went back to leading his old, misspent life? Doubt it. He'd just been hand-raised by the Son of God. I'm sure he became quite holy.

Maybe I need to be holy.

Our church is next to the Dairy Queen. That's how people know it—the DQ church. Just like there's the DQ hotel and the DQ gas station. It makes it easy to find.

Not being a regular attendee, I wasn't sure (a) if they

were open on Mondays; (b) if the pastor would be around; or (c) why in hell he would want to talk to me. But it seemed to make sense to try.

Pastor Bartlett is a short, short man. He probably got stuffed in plenty of garbage cans back in the day. He always stands at the door of the church and shakes everyone's hands as we're filing out, and I always feel like my grip is too hard for the little guy, and I'm a giant towering over him.

I had to lie to my mom. Again. I told her I was meeting Toomy and some other people at DQ after school, and since it was on the way back to her office, she had no problem dropping me there.

There were a few cars in the church parking lot. I didn't know if they belonged to the people who worked there or to people like me deciding today, November tenth, it's time for God.

I walked in.

It took a moment for my eyes to adjust. The only light was what was coming in through the stain-glassed windows. It looked really nice. Quiet and peaceful. Serene.

Holy.

There was no one around, so I just sat for a minute on one of the back pews and thought about what I was going to say—if Pastor Bartlett was even there at all.

Some older woman came in, and I got all flustered. "Um, hi, I was looking for Pastor Bartlett?"

"He's in his office," she said in a sweet voice. She noticed my crutches. "Are you all right?"

"Oh, yeah—just a . . . um, can you tell me where his office is?"

She pointed toward a side door. "Through there and across the courtyard."

"Would I be . . . bothering him?"

"No, honey. He loves to talk."

So I went. Across the sanctuary, out the door, across a courtyard filled with empty flowerbeds awaiting the snow. I found the office and went in. There was another woman behind a glass partition, and I knocked on it lightly to get her attention.

She wasn't as friendly as the other woman, but I didn't care. I was so nervous about talking to the pastor she could have pulled my hair and I wouldn't have noticed.

She asked me to sit, but I said I'd rather stand, and sort of gestured to my crutches. She seemed to understand. It took about five minutes before Pastor Bartlett came out to find me.

He smiled, like he knew me, even though there's no way he could.

He extended his hand and I shook it, afraid as usual that I might crush his bones. Although the truth is he has a pretty good grip for his size.

"How can I help you?"

"Um . . ." I glanced over at the woman behind the partition. She was watching. "Can we talk in private?"

"Certainly," he said, then led me to his office. "Campbell," he said when we were both seated. "Your parents are Ron and Gretchen?"

I nodded. My palms were leaking sweat.

"How old are you, Cara?"

My voice cracked. "Sixteen."

"Ah." He smiled and the smile was warm and seemed real. He folded his hands, set them in his lap, and leaned back in his chair. "So, Cara, how can I help you today?"

It took me a few moments to get started.

"I wanted to . . . um, I know this is probably a weird question . . ."

He just sat smiling, waiting.

"Okay, do you believe in resurrection?"

"Of course. Our savior is living proof."

"But I mean of . . . other people. Real people."

"Jesus was—"

"No." I waved my hands in the air. "Scratch that. What I mean is do you think people can still be resurrected today?"

"There are many stories of near-death experiences," he said. "At my former church I knew a man who had experienced that."

"Good. Okay. So that's real. What about reincarnation? Do you believe in that?"

It struck me that this was a pretty weird conversation to be having with someone I hardly knew, but then again, maybe that's what made it better. Once I was a few questions in, I wasn't so nervous anymore. I was talking to an expert.

Pastor Bartlett seemed to ponder it for a moment. Then he put his hands on top of his desk and leaned forward. "Cara, this is what I believe. I believe we can't put God in a box. We can't limit him. We can't say resurrection or reincarnation are the way God works, or the only way he works, or they can't possibly be the way he works. We humans like to make up stories about how we think God manages his business. We might be partially right, we might be completely wrong.

"I like to think of it this way," he continued, and I felt like he was making up a sermon on the spot, just for me. "I love the ocean. I love to stand on shore and watch the waves and listen to the music of them lapping at the sand. And I notice that as far as I look, all I can see is ocean. But I also know that that's not all there is of the ocean—it extends far beyond what I can see from where I stand.

"I think it's the same with God. We see part of what he does and we try to imagine everything else. We might be right in the things we guess, we might be wrong."

We both sat in silence for a while. I wanted to think that over before I asked him anything else.

"Have you ever known anyone who said they were reincarnated?"

"No."

"But you think it's possible."

"I think more things are possible than we know," he said.

I wasn't sure if I had gotten what I came for. I think I wanted more.

And then, without me even asking, he gave it to me.

"I don't think death has the last word, Cara. God has the last word. Always. People are so frightened of death. Why?"

Maybe it was a rhetorical question, but I wanted to answer anyway. "Because it's so . . . different. We know what it's like here, and even when it's not so great we at least know what to expect."

"Do we?" he asked. "I can't know what will happen in the next second, can I? The ceiling might fall in, you might start singing, I might get a craving for pizza—"

I had to smile. "Yeah, I guess that's true."

And then he said my favorite thing of all. "If you asked a baby still in the womb if it wanted to be born, it would say no. It has everything it needs—food, warmth, security. But the process of birth brings us into a whole new existence. And once we're here, we love it.

"How do we know it isn't the same with death?" he asked. "Maybe we can't imagine how wonderful it will be to go through the process and come out on the other side.

"I'll bet in my twenty-eight years of ministry I've attended the deaths of some two hundred people—just comes with the territory. And I can tell you without exception, every one of those people died peacefully in the end. Why? Because by the time they got there, death seemed as natural and as inviting as birth. How can we fear something when we know it comes from God?"

I nodded and just sat there. We didn't speak for a little while. It didn't feel uncomfortable to be silent. It was like sitting at the lunch table with David.

"Okay," I said, standing, "well, thanks for your time. This was really interesting."

He looked at me sort of strangely. "Is there . . . anything else you'd like to talk about?"

"No, that was it."

He shook my hand. "I look forward to seeing you again soon."

"Well, Christmas Eve for sure. We love that service."

"I give other good ones, too," he said with a smile.

I got all flustered. "Yeah, I'm sure you do, it's just that my parents—"

He patted me on the arm. "It's fine, Cara. Come whenever you like."

He escorted me back to the reception area. I was almost out the door before he asked, "Shall I pray for you?"

"Sure," I said, feeling uncomfortable. It was too personal, and that woman behind the glass was listening.

"Shall I pray anything in particular?" Pastor Bartlett asked.

I thought about it for a moment. "You can pray for my leg. It could use the extra help."

I walked out and took a few steps across the parking lot before I realized I didn't have a plan for getting home.

I pulled out my cell phone but didn't dial right away. Finally I got up the nerve.

"David? Can you possibly do me a favor?"

36

I enjoyed a chocolate dipped cone at DQ while I waited.

And wondered why he was even doing it. I mean, David made it pretty clear that he doesn't think much of me, and yet (a) I called him for a ride, and (b) he agreed.

I don't think it's my charms. Obviously it's not my charms. Or my looks—David seems pretty immune to both. I don't think he's the kind of guy who feels guilty, either, like he owes anyone anything—least of all me.

So why? And why did I even call him? It's easy to say because I have no more friends. Or because I didn't want to bother my mom at work or have her ask me questions like why Toomy didn't drive me home. The one thing that sucks extra hard about having my leg in this brace is that all that freedom I had for a few months after my birthday, getting to drive myself everywhere, ended much too soon. I know the day will come again when I can go wherever I want, whenever I want, but that day seems far away from where I'm sitting now.

So you could say David was my only choice. I suppose I could have skipped him and called one of his parents. They like me, don't they? But that seemed a little too familiar. You don't just adopt someone else's parents without explicit invitation.

So that's my explanation for me, but what about David? Why would he ever do me a favor after all the fights we've had?

Can't help you there, Cara. Move on to the next test question and come back to this one.

He pulled up in his beater two-door and didn't even look at me. I got in. This time he didn't help. It took me a while to maneuver my leg, my crutches, me into the back seat. When I stopped making grunting noises he must have figured I was done, because then he started driving.

I said, "I was thinking maybe I could help your parents a little more with their research. Are they home?"

"My mother's sick," David said.

"Sick how?"

"She thinks she caught whatever you have. She's been throwing up since this morning."

I was a little perturbed that Mrs. Mayer had told David that I threw up, but I didn't feel like explaining that I puked because of what I saw when Dr. Mayer hypnotized me—not because I was sick.

"Okay," I said, "then do you mind dropping me off home?"

David touched the brim of an imaginary cap. "Yes, madam." Like he was my chauffeur. Only it wasn't a friendly kind of kidding.

When he pulled into my driveway he actually turned off the car, came around, and helped me out. At first I thought, "Oh, that's nice—maybe he doesn't hate me so much after all," but then I got it.

He helped me all the way inside, and instead of leaving right away asked casually, "So . . . is Beth around?"

I narrowed my eyes. Does he think I'm stupid? I'd only told him that part about Beth saying she thought he was cute because I was trying to make a point about his personal hygiene. Typical guy, David only heard what he wanted to.

"She's only thirteen," I said.

David pretended not to understand. "I wanted to ask her something about—"

And just then Beth came down the stairs.

"Oh, hi," she said, smiling at David.

"Thanks a lot for the ride," I told him. Then I started herding him toward the door.

"I brought something for you," David told Beth. "Hold on." And he left to go out to his car.

"Why is he here?" Beth asked.

"To court you," I said. "Go back upstairs."

Beth laughed. "Seriously? Awww!"

David came back before I could convince Beth to disappear.

He held up a thick piece of sheet music. "I thought you might like this. I found it on a website for violin prodigies." He handed it to her, and Beth read it with excitement.

"I love this piece! I haven't played it for a while, but I think I still know it. Come upstairs. Want to hear it?"

"Beth!"

She shooed me off. "Come on," she told David. "We'll leave the door open," she told me, as if that made any difference. The whole point is she's too young—whether she's supervised or not.

I crutched up the stairs after them and made sure they knew I was right across the hall. Beth started playing almost right away. So at least I knew where her hands were.

As soon as she finished the piece, I showed up in her doorway. "Okay, then, well that was beautiful, but I know David needs to be going now. Thanks for the ride. Tell your mom I hope she feels better."

David wasn't moving. He stayed sitting on the floor with his back propped against Beth's bed, pretending to read some of Beth's music.

I whistled. "David. My parents don't let us have guys in our rooms."

"That is such a lie!" Beth said. "You had Alex up in your—"

"They don't let girls in *junior high* have guys in their rooms. Sorry," I said, motioning for him to go. "Up and out."

David gave me a strange sort of amused look. "What's the problem here?"

"The problem is I'm not letting you put the moves on my little sister. She's too young."

"He's not putting the moves on me," Beth said with embarrassment. "He's just listening to me play."

"She's giving a recital next month," I told him. "You can hear her then. We'll send you an invitation."

David took his time getting up from the floor. He handed Beth her music. "Thanks for the concert. You really play beautifully."

"Thanks," she said, obviously pleased.

"Okay, Mayer, let's go."

"Your sister's a tyrant," David told Beth.

"Yes, but we love her."

I didn't like at all this witty little repartee between the two of them. "Hey, lover boy, let's go."

At the door downstairs David turned to me with a smile. "I really make you nervous, don't I?"

"Anyone sniffing around my sister makes me nervous."

"Jealous?"

"Hardly!" I batted him with the end of my crutch. "I really appreciate the ride, but don't ever come back."

His smile evaporated. "You're a piece of work. Take, take, take. Whatever's good for you—right?"

"No. I've said about twenty times how much I appreciate the ride. But come on—a thirteen-year-old?"

"She said she turns fourteen in December."

"Oh, good for you. If we were in Ethiopia I'd say go for it. But we're not. My sister is off limits."

"You're the queen of the world?"

"When it comes to my sister, yes."

"And what if she doesn't agree?" David asked.

"You're pretty full of yourself, aren't you?"

David tipped his imaginary cap. "The servant will return to his quarters, Queen Cara. All the world revolves around you."

I hate when he acts like that. Like I'm being so unreasonable. Or stuck up.

"My parents don't let us date until high school."

David shrugged. "I just wanted to see what you would do. I'm not looking for a girlfriend."

"So you're leading her on?" I asked.

"I never said anything—you did. You're the one

calling me lover boy. All I wanted to do was give her a piece of music and see if she could play it. I happen to respect her talent. I'm sorry you don't."

"Right. You know me so well."

"Not everyone is as obsessed with sex as you are," David said.

I scoffed. "I am not obsessed with sex, and for the record, you're the one who admitted you think about it all the time, and you even think about it with me."

"No," he said calmly, "you asked me if I ever thought about it, and yes, I do—what seventeen-year-old guy doesn't? It's biology—look it up. And you asked me if I ever think about sex with you, and yes, I do, but also with half the girls at our school. It's natural. It's not personal. I don't personally want to date you or any other girl your age or type. It's nothing but a big drama with all of you." He did his best imitation of a girl. "'Oh, he said that, did he mean this? Should I break up with him? Does your boyfriend buy you presents? Why doesn't mine? Boo-hoo!'"

"That's not how—"

"The last thing I want," David went on in his normal voice, "is some temperamental, flighty girl telling me I don't comb my hair right or smell right or wear the right clothes or treat her the way all those magazines say I should be treating her. Not every guy worships you, Cara. We can think about what your breasts look like without ever wanting to spend even five minutes in a room with you."

We both glared at each other.

"You're a real jerk," I said.

"And you're the most conceited person I've had the pleasure to know."

"You're never going to get a girlfriend."

David laughed. "Have you not been listening? I don't want any of you stupid high school girls. You're bad news. You're a waste of time and money. I'm waiting until college when I can find someone with some depth."

"As if she'll have you," I said. "You think suddenly in college you'll blossom into this stud?"

"No," David said, "but I think maybe there will be more people than in Pinedale, and maybe even one or two will look beyond appearances and care about what's inside."

"What's inside is a rude son of a bitch."

"Always nice talking to you, Cara. Please don't think of me next time you need to use someone."

The second he was gone I went upstairs to do another workout on my arms.

Because one of these days I'm going to pummel that guy.

37

I got a note this morning from Ms. Josephson saying, "Victoria Toomy would like to meet with you in my office second period."

I wasn't sure if her dad put her up to it, or if she just decided on her own. But they couldn't force me to meet with her, right? If I'd just said no, what could they do? Drag me out of class and make me listen to Toomy whine about me?

The kid who'd delivered the message was waiting for my reply. Fine, I thought. Let her get it out of her system. Might as well get this over with.

So there we were second period, sitting across from each other in Ms. Josephson's cramped office, both of us with stern, snotty looks on our face, me wondering why I had ever agreed to it.

Ms. Josephson said, "Cara, Victoria tells me there's been some bad blood between the two of you lately, and she wants to work it out."

Toomy wouldn't meet my eye. I wondered if she was going to let Ms. Josephson do all the talking.

"Do you think that's true?" Ms. Josephson asked me. "Have you two had a falling out?"

"No," I said. "I'm not mad at her or anything. I just don't want to hang out anymore."

That got Toomy to look at me. "Why? Why're you being such a bitch all of a sudden?"

"Victoria," Ms. Josephson cautioned. "Let's not get into name-calling."

Toomy folded her arms across her chest. "Make her tell me why."

I laughed. "No one's going to make me—"

Ms. Josephson said, "I've found this works best when each party states what's on her mind. Then we can try to sort it out from there. But I'm not going to 'make' either of you."

Toomy and I both sat silent for a minute. I thought about just getting up and leaving.

"You're different," Toomy mumbled.

"Yes," I said, "I am."

"Why?"

"Because it was time to be different."

"What happened?" she said. "Ever since you came back to school—"

"No accusations," Ms. Josephson said. "Just stick to what you're feeling."

Toomy sighed. "I'm feeling that she's been a bitch to me ever since her operation. And she broke up with Alex and hates everybody now. I'm feeling like she's a bitch."

Ms. Josephson let that go. She could probably see there was no reforming Toomy in that short period of time.

Ms. Josephson turned to me. "Cara? How do you feel about what Victoria said?"

"I feel that I haven't been a bitch at all. If anyone's a bitch, she is, since she's the one going around calling me a bitch every time she sees me. I haven't called her anything. I've just been keeping to myself. And I'm sorry if that upsets people—" No, don't lie. "I'm not sorry if it upsets people, because they'll just have to learn to live with it. I have more important things to do now than hang around trashing people."

Now Toomy was warmed up. "Why am I your best friend one week and then suddenly I'm not?"

"Because I had some time to think."

"And you think you're better than me now?"

"No," I said, "I just want to be left alone."

"Then you're just a rank bitch."

I turned to Ms. Josephson. "See? This is why I knew it was pointless. I'm not having a fight with Toomy, I just don't want to be friends with her anymore."

"Fine, bitch!"

Ms. Josephson held up her hands. "Girls, let's settle down. Cara, is there something Victoria did?"

"No. It's just me. I've changed."

"And now you're so great," Toomy sneered.

"No, it's just that I don't want to spend my time doing the things I used to. It's not personal. I just want to be alone."

Toomy looked at Ms. Josephson for confirmation that I was a bitch. Ms. Josephson tapped her pencil against her lap and thought about her next move.

"Can you give Cara the space she needs?" she asked Toomy. "How about for a month?"

"I'll give it to her for forever," Toomy said. "I don't want to be her friend."

"Thank you," I said, and meant it. I almost wanted to shake Toomy's hand, but that would have totally confused her.

"Just stay away from me," Toomy said.

"I will." I didn't bother to point out that's exactly what I've been doing.

"My father's not going to invite your parents to any of the football dinners."

"Fine," I said. "I'll tell them that."

"I want all my clothes back," Toomy said.

It was just like a divorce. "I'll bring them tomorrow. Sorry, I forgot I still had some."

This wasn't going so badly after all.

But then Toomy had to say, "You owe Alex an explanation, too."

My face got hot. Amazing how fast anger can rise up in me. "Alex knows why."

"No, he doesn't," Toomy said. "I'm sick of him asking me."

I was SO tempted. The words were almost out of my lips. All it would have taken was a gesture—just point to one single body part—and even if Ms. Josephson couldn't have figured it out from that, she might at least have asked some questions. And then maybe the truth would come out. And then what would Toomy say? What would everybody say? And what would Alex do to get back at me?

"Can I go now?" I asked Ms. Josephson. She nodded, but I could see she wasn't exactly satisfied. She's probably had more success with other friend fights. But mending a friendship requires two people who want it back. I'm never going to be one of those people.

Toomy stayed behind in Ms. Josephson's office, no doubt to talk about me some more, which cracks me up considering how much smack Toomy has always talked about Ms. Josephson. Whatever. These people will all have to figure it out for themselves. I am not responsible for them.

As I made my way back to class, I tried to imagine what a session like that would be between me and David.

"David," Ms. Josephson would say, "Cara feels you have a completely false impression of her. She'd like to explain what she's about."

"I already know everything," David would say so smugly. "She represents everything I despise."

And yet he came when I called him for a ride. And he still talks to me sometimes, even though he keeps claiming he's done with me.

And he says girls are big drama queens? Girls are too hard to figure out?

His parents should do a study on him. NDE—not Near-Death Experience, but Nebulous David Explained.

38

I thought it was polite to ask. "How's your mother feeling?"

"Still sick," David said, not looking up from his book.

"Is she going to go to the doctor or anything?"

"Apparently. Thank you for your concern."

Jerk. Fine. I took my bagged lunch—an apple, a hunk of cheese, and a Hershey's bar with almonds—down to the opposite end of the table.

I was so absorbed in my own reading I didn't see David walk up to me. Lunch was almost over, and he had a message to deliver. "They said you can come over any afternoon this week. My mom's going to get some antibiotics today, and she wants to keep interviewing you while it's all fresh in your mind."

He said it like the whole thing was a bad taste in his mouth.

"Thank you," I said, but he was already walking away.

I wasn't going to wait. I wanted to talk to them as much as they wanted to talk to me. And considering how unfriendly David was the last time I asked him for a ride, I knew I'd have to make other arrangements. So once I was outside away from the lunchroom din I called my mother and asked her if she could take me over to David's after school—more studying.

"You seem to be spending a lot of time with this boy," she said. And she didn't sound very happy about it.

I could have set her mind at ease, but that would mean telling her the real reason I was going over there. Instead I just said, "Yeah."

"Can't he give you a ride?"

"Um, no, he has to leave early today. Can you just take me?"

One of the advantages to my mother always being so swamped at work is that sometimes, like this time, she couldn't give my lame story the time it deserved for examination. She was already talking to someone else who must have come in to her office. "Okay," she told me quickly, "see you then."

Since she's never actually met David, she didn't realize that was him pulling out of the parking lot just as she drove up to the curb. I took my time loading myself into her car so he'd have plenty of head start.

Once we reached his house, I reversed tactics and got out as quickly as I could, hoping no one would feel the need to come out and speak to my mother about the release form or anything else. I made it safely to the door and my mother drove off.

Dr. Mayer answered, and had a very funny look on his face.

"Oh, Cara." He glanced behind him. "Um, this isn't really a good time—"

"Tell her to come in," Mrs. Mayer called from the kitchen. "She might as well know."

Dr. Mayer gave me this uncharacteristically boyish smile. It was so undignified I didn't know how to react.

David was in the kitchen sitting across from his mother. He looked as unhappy as ever to see me walk in.

Which I was getting really sick of. "Never mind," I said, giving him my meanest look. "I'll come back some other time."

Mrs. Mayer's eyes were glistening. She threw up her hands like she was tossing confetti into the air. "I'm pregnant!"

"Wha-at?"

"Pregnant! Forty-four and pregnant! It's incredible!"

David didn't even pretend to look happy.

"That's wonderful!" I said. I gave her a hug, which she enthusiastically returned.

"Oh, Cara, you have no idea how miraculous this really is! After I had Jilly I had all sorts of problems, and they finally had to take out one of my ovaries. They said the other one was basically dead, so all this time I've been assuming—" She smiled and got all teary. "It's so wonderful!"

Dr. Mayer stood beside her, holding her hand.

"I'm so happy for you," I told them. "Congratulations!"

Dr. Mayer grinned at me like a kid.

"You, too," I told David. "Just think of having another—I mean, a little brother or sister."

He glared at me. He knew I wasn't stupid. He knew I could see how he felt.

He got up from the table and left the kitchen. His parents didn't seem to notice he had gone.

Dr. Mayer held out a chair for me. As soon as I sat down Mrs. Mayer patted my good knee.

"Babies come when they want," she told me. "Whether we're ready or not."

"But you're ready," I said. "Look how happy you are."

Dr. Mayer squeezed her hand and kissed her on the cheek. It was so sweet to see. Those two really love each other. I don't know if I've ever seen my parents holding hands. Although, to be fair, they might if my mom just found out she was pregnant. Then again, maybe not. I'm not sure she'd be as thrilled about it as Mrs. Mayer.

"How far along are you?" I asked.

"About a month, my doctor thinks."

"Congratulations," I said again. "This is really great."

"Cara," Dr. Mayer said, "I hope you don't mind, but I'm a little too agitated to work with you today."

"Oh, of course," I said. "Completely. I, uh, just need to give my mom a call—" Although the thought of going through the whole thing with her again wasn't very appealing.

"Davey can take you," Mrs. Mayer said.

"Oh no, I wouldn't want to—"

"Davey?" she called.

He didn't answer.

"Would you mind going up there?" she asked me. "I'd like to talk to Mark for a while."

"Of course," I said. "No problem."

So I climbed the stairs.

And discovered David's secret.

39

His room is huge—about twice as big as mine. The only furniture is a bed and a desk sitting out in the middle of the room. I could see his dresser inside the open closet. I understood immediately why he had put it there: he needed as much wall space as possible.

He was so absorbed in what he was doing he didn't hear me come in.

"Oh, my God."

He spun around. "Get out." He leapt up from his stool and came toward me and actually tried to push me—a poor defenseless gimp with a mean right cross if he really wanted to test me—out of his room.

"David, it's fantastic! Oh, my God—did you do all

this? Stop!" I yelled because he was still pushing and I was afraid he'd knock me off my crutches.

He realized what he was doing and came back to his senses.

"Get out," he still insisted.

"I can't," I said. "You're wonderful." And I have never meant that more.

David Mayer is not only a mathematical genius, he is also an artistic genius.

The wall I was staring at—the one he had been touching up when I came in—was Leonardo da Vinci's *The Last Supper*. Every detail and nuance of the original, reproduced there on a teenage boy's wall out of basic hardware paint. I saw the cans.

On the smallest wall, some intricate sketches of different body parts—shoulders, arms, hands, feet. I recognized *Vitruvius Man*, that famous da Vinci drawing of the ideal proportions of a man, with the guy looking like he's standing in a wheel with double arms and legs outstretched. There's a poster of that in the team trainer's office.

On the third wall, just to my right, another da Vinci —*The Virgin and Child with Saint Anne*. I know, because I looked it up tonight.

Each wall more spectacular than the next. Each one a perfect replica of da Vinci's paintings and drawings. Each one the work of an absolute master, and he's only seventeen.

"Oh, my God," I kept saying. I had to put my hand over my mouth to keep from saying it a hundred times more.

David finally broke in. "Fine. You saw it. Show's over." Once more he tried to hustle me out.

I felt both anger and awe. I pushed away his hands. "What is wrong with you? Why do you have to be such a freak all the time? Why can't I see this? Why aren't you showing everyone? You're an absolute genius! Do you know what people would give to be able to do something like this? Why can't you show it? Why do you have to be such a jerk all the time?"

Apparently my voice was a little louder than I thought, because Mrs. Mayer had to call from the kitchen, "Kids, everything okay?"

"Yes!" I yelled back. "Your son is a genius! He's brilliant! He's incredible! Seriously," I said, turning back to him, "you are really, really, REALLY good. You're fantastic. I can't believe you've been hiding this. You're amazing. I've never met someone so talented in my whole life."

He actually looked . . . pleased. But only for a second. Then it's like he caught himself—like he couldn't stand letting me compliment him. Or maybe he just didn't want me to think that anything I said might actually matter to him.

"Well, now you've seen," he said. "Thanks for stopping by." He reached back for the edge of the door and started to close it.

I blocked it with my crutch. "What is your problem? Talk to me! How long did it take you to do all this?"

He sighed like it took such an effort to be decent. "I don't know. A long time."

"And why aren't you showing this to people? Why does it have to be such a big secret?"

"Who would I show it to?"

"Me! Everybody!"

"And that would help me how?" David asked.

"Are you kidding me? People would see you're brilliant! They might even like you, you idiot. They'd think you were cool. You might actually have some friends."

"Oh, friends at Pinedale High. What an achievement."

"Why do you have to be such an ass all the time?" I said, my voice rising. I had to be careful, or Mrs. Mayer was going to call up there again. "Seriously, David. Maybe if you were a little bit nicer, people would actually like you."

"What people? Your little buddies in the brute squad? No, thanks."

"People like me, stupid. Normal people."

He laughed at that. "Oh, okay, right. Well, I think you've seen enough here."

Again he tried to crowd me out his door.

This wasn't going at all like it should have. I had

discovered something—something HUGE. And it was impressive. And I wasn't getting that across. I switched my tactics.

"David, you don't understand—girls would like this."

He scoffed. "What is it with you and girls? Why are you so concerned about my love life all the time?"

"Because I think I could help you."

"No, thanks," he said, any humor in his voice gone. "Why don't you just worry about your own very prestigious life? I'm sure that takes all your time."

SO frustrating, that guy. Do you know how many people would kill to have me take them under my wing? I could have girls hanging all over David in a week's time if he'd just cooperate.

"Shoo," he said, waving me out of there like I was a feral cat. "I'm sure my parents need you for something. I think they're channeling wolves today."

Which reminded me why I'd come up there in the first place. I was sure he wasn't in the mood to do me any favors, but I had to ask.

"Um, actually . . ." His expression told me I was right about his mood. But I pressed on.

"I hate to take you away from this—believe me, I want you to keep painting as much as you possibly can —did I mention you're freaking brilliant?—but your mom said to ask you . . . well, I think they wanted to . . . talk some more. You know, about the baby."

He stiffened at that.

"So, I know it's a huge imposition," I said sincerely, "but could you possibly give me a ride home?"

He sighed again. "You'll have to wait while I close up." He went back into his room to put lids on all the open cans, then took the brushes into his bathroom to clean them.

Leaving me alone. With all that glory.

And as I stood there and studied his walls, paint stroke by masterful paint stroke, I suddenly realized an essential truth: David's not the idiot, I am.

This is what it took death for me to see—that some guy I'd completely overlooked was secretly a genius painter I would have admired if I'd met him after seeing one of those beautiful walls. If someone had blindfolded me, told me they were going to show me the work of a great man, led me in here, done a ta-da and revealed all this glorious art, I would have begged to know what incredible specimen of a guy had been able to pull off something so spectacular.

And then if David Mayer had walked into the room —without me ever having met him, without me knowing anything about him but how talented he is— I'm sure I would have thought he was totally hot. I would have seen this guy who was all artsy-looking, with his deep brown eyes and scruffy jeans and black Converses and tousled hair. I would have flirted with him, put on my best show, done everything I could to get us together. I would have felt lucky to be seen with him.

Right. But that's not how it is, is it? Because I came at him from the wrong direction. I entered through the wrong door. And that totally messed up whatever chance I might have had to see him this other way.

David came out of the bathroom wiping the last bits of paint from his hands onto his jeans. He asked in his usual bored voice, "Ready?"

No. Not for any of this.

40

I waited until I had crammed myself onto his back seat and we were already a minute or two down the road. I knew I was probably pushing my luck, but suddenly I wanted to know a lot more than I did about David. "Can I ask you something?"

"No."

"Too bad," I said, faking confidence, "I'm asking. Why are you such a—" I thought better of how I was going to phrase it. I actually wanted to know the answer to this, and insulting him probably wasn't going to get me anywhere. "Why are you so against what your parents do?"

At first I thought he was going to give me the silent treatment again. But apparently he was just formulating the answer.

"Tell you what," he said. "You take your perfectly normal existence—nice, normal, rational parents—and suddenly throw reincarnation and angels and spirit guides and all that crap into the mix. Then you have your parents decide—for *you*, with no real consultation —that it would be better for the family—no, correction: maybe some spirit guide *said* it would be better for the family—if we all left our happy, regular life in Denver and instead moved out to the world's most moronic town—"

I let that go. I didn't dare interrupt what I was sure was going to be a very revealing rant.

"—so we can all commune with nature and be all spiritual, you understand, and meanwhile you've left behind every friend you ever had— 'Oh, sweetie, there's always e-mail,' as if that was going to work—and you have to start over at Jock High, where the closest thing that passes for an intelligent conversation is people talking about how much hair can grow on their backs before someone starts testing them for steroids—"

No one is taking steroids. But I let that go.

"—and the girls—the ones you're so concerned about—are all plastic-looking airheads or Jockettes like you who have arms as big as my thighs—"

Thanks for noticing.

"—or you've got your psychopathic paste-eaters who would probably carve a guy's name onto their foreheads—"

Yeah, there is that girl Sonia—

"—and the only movie theater in town shows nothing but car chases and slasher films and there's only one bookstore, but eighteen different sports shops—"

Five.

"—and meanwhile your psychiatrist father and trial attorney mother have left their respectable, normal practices in an exciting, cultural town so that instead they can spend all their time walking in the woods and talking to angels or God or whoever it is and trying desperately to communicate with your dead little sister, and meanwhile some beauty queen from school keeps telling you if you'd just smile a little more and start acting like the clones, and maybe bring a few tours through your bedroom every night so people can make fun of what you do and rob you of the one last pleasure in your life—then finally—*finally*—everything would work out perfectly well and everything would be fixed and everyone would be happy, the end." Finally he stopped to take a breath. "So, what do you say, Cara? Ready to trade places with me?"

I held it in as long as I could. But finally I couldn't help it. I burst out laughing.

"Yeah, well, glad you're so entertained," David said, but he sounded tired more than mad. "It's not quite so funny from my end."

"I'm sorry," I said, and I meant it. "It really does

sound awful when you put it that way. It's just that . . . you are kind of funny sometimes."

"Ha, ha."

We were both silent for a few moments, but I wasn't quite through. Somehow it seemed like his defenses might be down enough for me to slip in one more burning question.

"Can I ask you something else?"

"No."

"Why aren't you happy your mom is pregnant? That seems like some pretty great news."

"How is that great? She's going to kill herself. She's too old."

"No, she's not," I said. "I've heard of actresses having babies into their fifties."

"With surrogate eggs," David said. "And all sorts of medical procedures. It's not safe for regular people."

"You don't know that." Although it sounded like he did.

"Don't you ever read the papers?" David asked. "The older you get, the more complications you have. Women her age can have strokes or bleed to death, and their kids come out with all sorts of birth defects. It's a mess. She should just abort."

"She's never going to abort!"

And that's when it hit me. I remembered the last time I'd had a discussion about that.

"Hold on—when did she say she got pregnant?"

"I don't know," David said, clearly not enjoying the conversation. "About a month ago."

A sick chill went through me. "I wonder which day."

"I don't know," David said sarcastically. "Why don't you ask her the last time she had sex?"

That wasn't a bad idea. Weird, but not a bad idea.

I whipped out my phone.

"What are you doing?" David said. "You're not actually going to ask her?"

I was. I did. Mrs. Mayer hesitated at first, because it is an awfully strange question for an outsider to ask, but the fact is she had already figured out the exact date, and she told me.

I'm sure my face was chalk white.

I couldn't talk to David about it. Knowing how he feels about his parents' work, there's no way he'd want to hear it.

And I couldn't call back and tell Mrs. Mayer. It's too weird. I'd never told her the date of my surgery—it just hadn't been important. Now I wasn't sure how she'd react.

And that left only one person: Beth. Because of all the people in my life right now, she is the only one I can really trust with the truth.

I'd sort of tested her out with the sex thing, and even though I didn't know I'd ever be having this conversation with her, I knew that it would be all right. Beth could handle it. And moreover, Beth would listen with an open mind, and might see it the way I did.

I thanked David for the ride and crutched into the house as fast as I could. My parents still wouldn't be home for another hour. If I talked fast I might get it all out.

I took the stairs too quickly and ended up bumping my leg, which felt less than good, but there was no time to waste.

"Beth, we have to talk."

She stopped mid-bow on whatever piece she was practicing.

"I've been keeping something from you," I said, "but now it's even bigger than I thought, and I have to talk to someone about it, and it has to be you. So come on." I motioned her over to her bed and settled onto it myself.

"Hold on." She put her violin back in the case and went over to her dresser. "I was saving this for later, but we might as well have it now." She fanned across the bedspread five new bars of German chocolate. "Take your pick. Start talking."

I love my sister. I unwrapped one of the bars with hazelnuts and got right to it.

"I woke up while I was dead," I told her. "And here's what happened."

41

My time was up. My heart was a fraction of a second from beating again.

I was almost sad to leave.

We were still sitting on the bench, staring out at the nothing of the gray.

"You'll be fine," the woman told me, as if she read my mind.

"I don't know what to do," I said.

"You'll know."

She tapped my chest, and the yellow light burned bright.

I waited, too nervous to ask her anything else.

Then I felt the pull of my body—the irresistible pull. It wanted me back and I wanted to go. I wanted to go so much. The feeling was sweeter than I can describe.

Like finding something lost after searching so very long.

I was already slipping away when I heard her say one more thing.

"Cara, look for me."

42

"Oh, my God," Beth said. "Do you really think it's her?"

"Who else could it be?"

Beth clutched her arms. "That gives me chills. Are you going to tell them?"

"No! I don't think so. Do you think I should?"

"You can't," Beth said. "You'll freak them out."

"But Dr. and Mrs. Mayer know all about this stuff. Don't you think they'll be happy?"

"Would you?" Beth asked. "If I came to you and said, 'Hey, by the way, I already met your new daughter and wow, is she super tall'?"

We both sat there and thought about it for a minute. I cracked open another bar of chocolate.

"I think I have to tell them."

"What if you're wrong?" Beth asked. "Maybe it's just a coincidence—"

"There are no coincidences. Mrs. Mayer says so."

Beth shook her head. "I think you're tampering with the future. Don't all the books say you shouldn't do that?"

"What books?"

"You know, science fiction."

"Beth, I'm serious. This is real life."

She sighed. "I have no idea what you should do. This is the weirdest problem I've ever heard of."

The door opened downstairs. It was probably my mother.

"You can't tell anyone," I said.

"Who am I going to tell?"

"Mom, Dad, your friends—"

Beth reached over and squeezed my hand. "I will take this to my grave." She smiled. "And beyond."

43

I couldn't wait any longer. If there was any chance I could remember something more from when I was dead, I wanted to know it today.

Then I could figure out what to do.

I called the Mayers from school to make sure they could see me this afternoon. At least this time I didn't have to trick my mother into taking me over there. I told her I'd be catching a ride with David. Not that I'd asked him yet.

He seemed strangely shy around me today. Like I'd seen him naked or something. I guess in some ways I have.

"How's your mom feeling?" I asked at lunch.

"Vomitous."

He didn't fight me on the ride. Maybe he's finally

gotten used to me being around his house. But he still didn't feel the need to talk to me on the way over. Just when I thought we were making progress.

Mrs. Mayer didn't look so hot. She was wearing sweat pants and an old sweat shirt, and her face looked sweaty, too. No point in putting on makeup if you're just going to puke it off.

She smiled weakly. "Hi, Cara. Don't know how long I'll last. I may just have to set up the camera and fly."

As if to prove her point, she turned and fled to the bathroom and started making the most horrendous sounds. Poor woman. Why do babies do that to their mothers?

So while poor Mrs. Mayer kept retching, Dr. Mayer and I moved to the office.

I settled onto the couch and pulled the afghan over my legs.

"It probably won't take as long for you to go under this time," Dr. Mayer said. "It gets easier every time you do it."

He was right. A few sequences counting backward, his soothing voice guiding me, and I was back.

But not where I meant to be.

I wanted to go to the gray space. I wanted to revisit that last moment, to see if the woman said anything else that might confirm my suspicions. I wanted to hear it again—*Cara, look for me.* I wanted to tell her I'd found her. But that's not how memory works.

Instead my brain traveled backward further. Back to where I didn't want to go.

I saw the fuzzy outlines of the farm, and tried to tell Dr. Mayer no—*No—please, not there—*

But it was too late. I was back in Oklahoma.

It was later. I wasn't pregnant anymore. I was thin and looking so old and exhausted, with dark circles under my eyes. But Alex's mother was still there, so not that much time could have passed. She was already older than dirt the first time I saw her.

And someone else was there, too.

David.

David.

Did I say that out loud? *David.*

44

<hr>

He hauled in an armful of wood.

And we locked eyes.

That's how I knew. His eyes may have been blue in that life instead of brown, and his face and body may have looked like they belonged to a completely different man, but it was David. That was his soul looking out at me. And my God, the way he looked at me—

It was like getting slammed to the ground by an avalanche.

No, not an avalanche. That would have been too easy—I would have been out of my misery far too soon. This was more like being buried alive in slow motion, one shovelful of dirt at a time, the weight of it slowly crushing me to death. Because there, standing in the doorway, looking at me in a way I never thought anyone in my life would ever look at me, was a man who was not my husband and who I knew my husband would kill if he ever saw looking at me that way. Or the way I looked back at him.

The old woman was no fool. "Henry, git," she snapped. "Go fetch your brother. Louisa, get supper on."

Henry—David—didn't say anything. He just kept his eyes on me. I know because I—I mean Louisa—was gazing back at him the whole time.

I couldn't believe it: Louisa was in love. Not little puppy love, not lustful love, but that deep soulful love you read about and can't imagine ever actually experiencing. Well, I was experiencing it all right. And it hurt so much I could barely breathe. Because the whole time I was thinking if only I could just have a moment alone with him—if I could kiss him and hold him, even just for a second—I'd be so happy I might actually burst into flames.

"Go on!" the old woman shouted at him again.

This time David reluctantly left.

I wanted to run after him. Run screaming and crying to be free of that place and free to be with him. The ache for David hurt more than anything Alex had ever done to me—like my heart was already so thin and wispy, so full of holes, the only way I could possibly save it from shriveling up and dying inside my chest was to follow that man who had just walked out of my miserable house and spend the rest of my life with him, no matter how short that might be.

What had happened since I last saw Louisa? What was all this?

The old woman turned her vicious attention to me. "Get back to work, cow."

I almost laughed out loud—me, the one watching. The thin little weed of a young woman I was back then could hardly be called a cow. Especially by a woman as fat as Louisa's mother-in-law.

But I held my tongue. I knew I had to be careful around her. Whatever had just gone on, I knew that old bitch would have no trouble reporting it to my husband. I had to be more careful around David—I couldn't look at him the way I just had. And he certainly couldn't keep looking at me that way.

I worked in silence, loading wood into the stove, stirring a pot of what looked like beans and meat that sat on top of it.

Alex stomped in, reeking of sweat and booze. David followed a few steps behind, carrying in more wood. This time he kept his gaze to himself, and got busy stacking logs in the corner.

I was so distracted by him I didn't notice Alex behind me until he cupped his hand over my breast. I jumped. Alex squeezed harder. So hard my eyes watered. I couldn't look at David. I hoped he wasn't watching.

Alex whispered roughly, "Come out to the barn."

Now the tears really were flowing. But I nodded. Because that was my life.

As I made my way slowly for the door, I felt something tug me back.

A small hand gripped the hem of my dress.

I knelt and hugged the little girl to me. "Sweetie, Momma's gotta go for a while. Be a good girl?"

"No," the little girl sniffled.

"C'mon," Alex ordered.

"Just a minute," I answered hoarsely. I turned back to my girl. And looked into her eyes.

And I knew her.

My daughter had blue eyes and blond hair just like Alex, but I knew her. I knew her when she'd had brown eyes and long brown hair. I knew her at the most important moment in my life.

She was the woman from the gray space.

45

I gasped awake, like I'd just rescued myself from drowning.

"Cara?" Dr. Mayer said. "Are you all right?" He knelt beside me and took my pulse.

No, I wasn't all right. My body was drenched in sweat, I was cold, I was shaking—far from all right.

"You came out on your own," he said. "Can you tell me what happened?"

I shook my head. The tears were starting to flow in this life, too. I couldn't stand it anymore. It was too awful. Her life was too awful.

Dr. Mayer helped me sit up. He wrapped the blanket tighter around me and handed me a glass of water. I took a few sips.

"Can you talk?" he asked.

I took a breath and nodded.

"What happened? The last thing you said was 'You.' What did you see? Who was it?"

It took me a while, but I told him everything. Turns out I hadn't said David's name out loud after all—I'd been calling him Henry—so that was as much of a shock to Dr. Mayer as the rest of it. When I told him about the woman from the gray space, he sat back on his heels and swiped a hand over his forehead.

"Extraordinary."

What would he say if I told him the rest of it—that I knew where the woman was now? Just a few feet down the hall probably still making her mother throw up every last inch of her guts?

"I need to rest," I said.

"Would you like me to leave you alone?"

I nodded. Dr. Mayer turned off the camera. Until that moment, I didn't realize it was still running.

"Does . . . David never looks at those, does he?"

"No. I told you, Ginny and I keep confidential whatever happens during your sessions. We'll use your story, but we'll change all the names—including yours."

I nodded. My head was throbbing. I took a longer drink of water, then eased back onto the couch. Dr. Mayer turned down the light and gently closed the door behind him.

And then I could cry.

What a miserable, horrible life.

What had poor Louisa ever done to deserve that? More important, what had *I* ever done? Because wasn't this me? Wasn't this my poor soul enduring all that suffering?

I thought I knew what it was like to feel pain. I've broken bones, I've torn ligaments, I've been slammed and cracked and shoved and kicked, and I've shaken it off and gone on because it's just sports, right? It's just life.

But Louisa's kind of pain—that was on a whole other level. There was the physical—Alex's assaults, Alex's beatings—but the pain she felt down deep in her soul was so much, much worse. She wanted to die. She wished she had never been born. But at the same time she desperately loved her child, and now desperately loved David, and so she fought to stay safe and alive.

Desperate was the word. That described her whole life.

Wouldn't it be better if I didn't know any of this stuff? Wouldn't my life be a lot happier if I could just keep breezing along, never knowing I'd once been that wretched, lonely, abused young woman? What good does it do to learn the truth?

And what am I supposed to do with all this information now that I have it? I can't go back and fix Louisa's life for her, can I? I'm just watching—I'm not a player. It's like screaming at the TV when your team is down. *"Throw it! Shoot! SHOOT!"*

I wish I could shoot. Alex, I mean.

And that gave me an idea.

46

"Dr. Mayer? Can I talk to you?"

David was in the kitchen, too. My skin felt electric around him. I couldn't look at him for longer than a glance because I was afraid how I would feel.

It was all so weird.

Here I was, about to send myself back to where Louisa was dying of love for this man, and he was already there right in front of me, calmly eating an apple and doing his homework, and acting like I meant nothing more to him than an irritation and a distraction.

For a scary second I almost forgot about asking Dr. Mayer to come back with me to his office, and almost invited David instead. There in the dark I could have given Louisa exactly what she hoped and prayed for in her otherwise hopeless life. I could have told David it was his job to shut up for a moment, and then wrapped myself around him and made him give Louisa that kiss she wanted so desperately. I could have handed her the lips she hungered for, the body she wanted to hold, the breath she longed to feel against her face.

All for my Louisa.

But of course that was crazy. I wouldn't get a step past, *"Shut up and take it."* David would push me off him and storm out the door and leave me feeling humiliated. Which wouldn't exactly make this already-abused soul thank me for my efforts.

I cleared my throat. "I'm ready to go back."

"No, Cara," Dr. Mayer said. "It's too soon."

"I have to know what happens. It's too painful otherwise."

That got David's attention. I couldn't meet his gaze. I have the feeling from now on I'm always going to feel like it's Louisa looking back at him.

I cleared my throat again. "Please."

Dr. Mayer thought about it for a moment before answering. "Ginny said she's feeling better. Should I ask her to join us?"

I nodded. He left to go find her.

And there was that electricity again.

I couldn't help it—the Louisa part of me couldn't believe we were finally alone. *I should say something! This is it!*

Down, girl.

My breath was uneven. I switched to breathing out of my nose so he wouldn't hear it.

And then I realized how completely ridiculous I was being. Isn't David Mayer the most oblivious guy on earth? He wasn't going to notice my breathing or anything else about me. What did I have to be afraid of?

"So," he said, "has the wolf clan made you their queen yet?"

"What?" I was starting to feel more like myself already.

"Or are you an Inca princess this time?"

"Shut up, please." The headache was coming back. And I was tired of hunching over my crutches. "Tell your dad I went back to his office." The thought of lying on the couch in the dark again sounded pretty sweet.

"It's not real, you know," David said. "I hate to see you get so worked up for nothing."

"I'd listen to you if you knew the slightest bit about what you were talking about."

"People always like to believe they were Cleopatra or Joan of Arc or Alexander the Great in some previous life," David said. "Hell, I'd like to believe I was da Vinci." He leaned forward. "But it's *fantasy*, Cara. There's only one real world, and this is it." He leaned back again. "Hate to break it to you, but you seem like a good kid."

That was it. I was in no mood for his smugness and sarcasm and nasty personality. Louisa might have been in love with some previous version of David Mayer, but the current model was a jerk.

"Interesting you should say that," I said. "Because I just had the weirdest experience of having wild, crazy sex with you in a previous life. But I guess that never happened. You seemed pretty happy, though. I think you actually passed out."

David laughed. "Very Freudian."

"You were very inexperienced—I had to show you where everything went."

"I'm sure you did."

Why did that make me blush? This wasn't going the way I meant it to.

"Cara?" Dr. Mayer poked his head around the doorway. "We're ready for you. Ginny's in my office."

"Great. Thanks." I felt flustered. And stupid David was just grinning at me.

"You're an idiot," I told him.

"All hail, mighty Cleopatra."

I felt desperate now, too—desperate to crack him across the face with one of my crutches.

I forced myself to sound cocky. "You don't know what you're missing."

"Thanks for showing me the ropes," he said, turning back to his homework. "I'm sure I really appreciated it."

No way Louisa was going to end up with that man. Not if I could help it.

47

Five minutes. That's all they could count on.

The old woman slept until dawn every morning. Alex/Charles, Louisa, and David/Henry rose half an hour earlier to begin their chores. And sometime during that half hour Charles would go to the outhouse. Leaving Henry and Louisa alone.

"Are you all right?" Henry whispered. Louisa nodded. He stroked her cheek with his rough, warm hand. Louisa closed her eyes and leaned into it.

Henry brushed his lips against her temple, then softly kissed her ear. "I love you."

"I love you, too," she whispered.

This was always the best part. Until he came to live with them, Louisa hadn't heard those words since she last saw her parents, years ago. Her daughter Annie said

"Love you, Momma" in her own sweet little voice, but it wasn't the same.

Henry's lips moved to hers. He kissed her softly at first, then more insistently, his breath warm against her mouth. He held her so gently—nothing at all like Charles—but the kiss was always so brief. They drew apart sooner than either wanted to, and continued to speak in low voices. If Charles came in, they could quickly resume their work in the barn—Louisa milking the two cows, Henry raking the stalls.

They had no money. They both depended on Charles. They had nowhere to run to, and so never spoke of it. I know because I looked around inside her head. I asked her all those questions and more—*Why did you marry Charles? Why don't you fight back? Why won't Henry save you?*

I also asked how far it had gotten between her and Henry. They had only ever kissed. And that was more than enough for Louisa. Sex wasn't something she viewed as recreation. What she wanted was love.

I stayed inside her head. I wanted to do something for her. That was what I'd realized in the Mayers' kitchen—maybe if I went back, I could help her. I could give her the kind of strength she so obviously needed. Maybe that was what the woman in the gray space had tried to tell me—maybe this life as Louisa was the one where I'd lost my courage, and now it was time to bring it back.

"I love you so much," David/Henry murmured, his chin resting on my shoulder.

"I love you, too, Henry." I wanted to say more—tell him we should run away together, tell him we should leave right away—but the words wouldn't come. Because this wasn't me. I might have been inside Louisa's head, but it was her life, not mine. I could only watch what was already going to happen.

Henry reached for my hand. "Louisa . . ."

Little Annie sat nearby on a stack of hay, sleepily singing to herself. Suddenly the music stopped. That's how I realized Charles had found us.

I turned just as he swung.

48

I wish I could say I died quickly. I wish I could say it was over as fast as my own death in the operating room, but it wasn't like that this time. I felt it. Every blow. Felt the breath shocked out of my body and the blood flowing warm down my cheek. Felt the pain searing through my head, through my body, through my mind. I knew it was over. I knew I was about to leave them—the only two people I loved on that earth—and there was nothing I could do to stop it.

They tried, too. Little Annie scratched and bit, but he just kicked her out of the way. David shouted and pulled and hit, but Alex was so much bigger than all of us. Everything I'd always been afraid of if I'd refused him—if I'd run away—if he'd found us—this was it, and it was so much worse than I'd imagined.

A body can't last forever. And mine was a small and fragile thing. Finally I slipped away, racing toward the gray space, with my soul screaming that I didn't want to go.

This was finally a life I had learned to want, and now it was already over. As I sped upward, my heart felt torn to shreds. It was worse than any physical pain I'd just endured.

I tried to call their names, but no sound carried down. I wanted them to know I never meant to leave them—not now, not ever. I wanted to tell them I would have endured anything just to stay with them. I had made a mistake. I had been careless. I'd been too weak to fight back. I'd made so many mistakes, and now it was too late to ever be happy.

But they were already gone. I was already gone.

I was in the gray space again, alone this time. I wasn't ready for anything else. I wasn't ready to play a card game, or get on with a new life. I wanted my baby. I wanted David. I had lost everything I ever loved.

I wasn't strong enough.

I didn't get away soon enough.

I wasn't brave enough.

I woke up sobbing.

49

It took much longer to recover than before. Dr. Mayer said that's because this time I witnessed my own death.

Even though Mrs. Mayer looked like death warmed over herself, she still tried to console me with water and hugs.

"What was the point?" I asked them. "Why did I even have to have a life like that? It was horrible! It was all such a waste."

"There's a purpose to each life," Mrs. Mayer said gently, "no matter how tragic or short it seems. Mystics believe that with each incarnation, the soul takes on a new body to learn the specific lessons offered by that life. So it might switch genders, or skin colors, or be healthy one life and disabled the next—or abused, like you were. It all depends on what that particular soul needs to learn to progress further along in its journey."

I didn't know what to make of any of it. I was so completely exhausted. And all I could keep thinking about was how I hadn't been able to do anything to save her. Maybe if I'd just tried harder. Maybe if I hadn't been so swept up in the moment with David I would have heard Alex come in. Maybe if I'd been more careful—

No, that's bull. Alex was going to discover them one of those days. They were already being reckless. The real problem was in marrying Alex at all. What was Louisa thinking? Had she met both brothers before? Couldn't she see David was the better choice—the only real choice? And even if she hadn't met David before she married Alex, she should have taken Annie and run away with him afterward. They could have made it—he could have found work somewhere, they could have gone back to her parents—something. Anything but stay there and let Alex do that to her every day.

"Do you think we get to correct our mistakes?" I asked Mrs. Mayer. "If we meet the same people in our current lives?"

"Yes. That's one of the ways we progress." Then she ran off to puke some more.

"Can I . . . is David here?" I asked Dr. Mayer. Suddenly I knew there was no one I wanted to see more.

"Upstairs. But maybe you should rest a little more—"

"No, I'm fine. I need to ask David something."

It took me a while to negotiate the stairs. I really was drained.

His door was open. I sagged against the frame. "Hey."

He glanced back at me, then kept painting. He was touching up one of the disciples at the Last Supper.

He didn't invite me in, but I couldn't wait for that. I saw one specific place I needed to be, and right away. I crutched over to his bed and collapsed back onto his pillow.

"Rough session?" he asked, and not with his usual sneer.

"You have no idea." I lay there with my eyes closed, savoring the silence David always offered. I breathed in the scent of paint. And the scent of David on his pillow.

I was having a problem. This David, that David— not quite clear on the separation yet. I had come up there because I was in love and missing my lover. But it was like reading some romance novel and wishing I could be with the hero—it wasn't real. This was David Mayer, not David/Henry, and nothing I had just experienced—good or bad—bore any relation to my real life. For which I was deeply grateful in many respects.

But the feeling still lingered. David's warm lips, his

rough hand against my cheek, his breath against my skin, that soft, sad "I love you"—

STOP.

My eyes flew open. This wasn't healthy. My mind was seriously doing the loop-de-loop. I needed to get a grip.

My gaze settled on the ceiling. "Hey, what's that?"

David looked where I was pointing. "Night sky."

"But it looks . . . real."

"Nah, it's about two weeks off," he answered. "I need to repaint it."

Who was this guy? This wasn't Henry, this was David 2.0.

Maybe.

"Can I ask you something?"

"No," we said together, because I knew that would be his answer.

And true to form, I continued. I propped myself up on my elbow and watched him work for a few moments. Then I gave it a try.

"What if we start over?"

He didn't answer. At first.

"Start over how?" He kept painting.

"Start over by not being so nasty to each other."

"I don't recall ever being nasty to you," he said. "If there's any of that, you started it."

"You're claiming you're always nice to me?"

Silence.

"Like that," I said when a sufficient time had gone by. "Are you familiar with conversation? I say something, you say something—"

He turned around on his stool. "Cara, what do you want?"

There it was—that unnerving way he has of looking me right in the eye.

I resisted the urge to look away. I had to hold my ground.

"Is it possible you would ever like me?" I asked. And immediately I felt how pathetic that was. Since when do I beg?

David continued looking right at me. I watched his face for any sign . . . of anything—anger, scorn, sarcasm, joy—anything. Please.

"Yes." Then he turned around and went back to work.

ARRRR! "David. Look at me, please."

He turned around, but this time he was smiling.

"Truce?" I asked.

"If we must."

I let out a breath and fell back onto his pillow. "Everything about you is difficult. I need a nap now."

And apparently I wasn't kidding. Because when I opened my eyes again, the room was dark and the stars above the bed were glowing.

For a moment I had no idea where I was. But then I saw the thin light in the corner where David sat propped against the wall reading by the light of his booklamp.

"What time is it?" I asked.

"Around nine."

"Are you kidding? I need to get home."

"I'll take you," he said, getting up.

That little truce talk seemed to have done some good.

I felt stiff and sore sitting up. I still wasn't totally recovered from my death as Louisa.

"Can you hand me my crutches?" I'd thrown them out of reach when I collapsed onto his bed.

He brought them to me and I couldn't resist. Yeah, it was taking advantage of the situation, but after the day I'd had, I was entitled.

I stroked my hand over the top of his. His skin was as warm and smooth as it looked. Nothing at all like Henry's.

Except Henry's lips. Those had been soft and warm, too.

But I wasn't going to try that.

50

W e were quiet the whole ride home. As usual.
And this time David helped me out of his car,
just like he had that first time he drove me back to my
house. The time when I realized he wasn't like Alex
because he wouldn't think to scoop me up in his arms
and carry me upstairs and try to get me into bed.

While I waited for him to take out my crutches, I
leaned against his car and tipped my head back to look
at the stars. The real stars.

"Pretty good," I said, pointing upward.

"Yeah, I just redid them."

"Glow-in-the-dark paint."

"Of course," he said. "Otherwise what's the point?"

I smiled. He could be charming when he wanted
to be.

So could I.

"I feel like maybe you didn't take me seriously before," I told him. "I really do think you're incredibly, massively talented. I'm so deeply impressed by you."

"I took you seriously," he said.

"Okay."

It was cold and I wasn't dressed for it.

"Okay," I said again, knowing I needed to get inside, but not really wanting to.

"Is Beth home?" David asked.

"Why?" I said a little too harshly.

David chuckled. "Just checking."

He leaned against the car, a few inches away from me, arms crossed over his chest. He stared into the night sky.

I could hear myself breathing. My body flushed with warmth at the thought of the risk I was about to take.

I bumped my arm lightly against his. "You like me a little, right?"

Silence. While my heart pumped ridiculously hard.

Then finally, "A little."

I let out a breath. "Okay," I said for the third time. I had nearly perfected the word by then.

Time for one last bold move. I reached down and grasped a handful of fabric at the bottom of his hoodie. I pulled him toward me so slightly, so imperceptibly, I didn't want him to realize I had really done it.

And he didn't.

"See you tomorrow," he said.

"Oh. Yeah, okay."

I paused just in case he might realize too soon the opportunity he'd lost.

"Okay, see ya." I let go of his hoodie and started the slow crutch up to my door.

Behind me I heard his car door slam. The engine turned over, and that was it.

Idiot.

51

Maybe it was pathetic.

But with a guy like that, sometimes you have to spell it out.

"Hey, David?" I said as soon as his dad got him to the phone. "I'm really sorry, but I think I left something in your car. Would it be possible for you to come back?"

"What did you leave?"

I'd already thought of that. "It's . . . kind of embarrassing. I think it must have slipped out of my pocket under the seat or something. Would you . . . I'm really sorry, but can you come back?"

It gave me time to brush my teeth and put on a warmer top. I could have used a shower, too, since my time with Louisa and Alex had me sweating right through my clothes, but I just freshened up my deodorant and let it go at that.

I waited for him outside. I sort of had a plan, but I was also willing to wing it.

First I had to pretend to root around under his back seat. "Hm. Nope. That's weird—it must have fallen out somewhere else."

He leaned back against his car while he waited, and went back to studying the stars. This time his arms hung at his sides.

I shut the door and leaned next to him. I was afraid to breathe. I wasn't sure if this would work.

I moved a little closer—just close enough that our arms barely brushed against each other.

I sighed. "David, I'm really sorry."

He didn't say anything.

Again, I had to do all the heavy lifting.

I'd prepared a sort of speech, but at that moment it just seemed too . . . prepared. And I didn't need a speech as much as I needed to just tell the truth.

"I think I really misjudged you. And treated you like crap."

I moved half a millimeter closer. Our arms were warm against each other.

And then I took that extra step. I reached down and twined my pinky around his.

David let out a breath. I held steady and kept my finger on his.

My voice felt thin and weak. "I have changed, you know."

"Hm." His hand hadn't moved. But at least he hadn't drawn it away.

What was wrong with me? Since when was I so meek and insecure? Yeah, I was different, but I wasn't this girl—she was as skittish as Louisa.

"I'm going to do something now," I announced.

"What's that?" he asked in his same old bored tone, but this time it seemed forced.

"I might kiss you."

"Hm," he answered, like it wasn't really his concern.

"Because I really like you."

He didn't answer. But he bent his pinkie over mine, and that was good enough.

When the starting gate opens, you just have to go. If you hesitate—even for a hairy split-second—you've already lost the race. So I rolled toward him and didn't hesitate.

I was wrong about what I told him.

David Mayer knows how to kiss.

I didn't have to teach him a thing.

52

Talk about the starting gate. It's like David had just been waiting for the word. As soon as my lips hit his, I realized he was as hungry for me as I was for him.

And here's the difference: David took care of me.

The side of the car was too cold, so he stayed pressed up against it and rolled me over so I could lean into him. Which I did, body to body, mouth to mouth. He's the perfect height for kissing. He's the perfect a lot of things for kissing.

It wasn't like with Alex—in no way was it like with Alex. David didn't press or grope or rush. He treated me the way he treated Louisa—softly, tenderly, but with so much passion I couldn't believe this was David

Mayer I was kissing. He was the hottest thing I've ever experienced.

The crutches got in our way, so I let those go and he supported my weight. He kept one hand on the small of my back, one behind my neck, and it gave him perfect access to all the parts of me he was kissing: my lips, my cheeks, my ears, my throat . . .

It was the kiss Louisa longed for every day, with one huge difference: we had all the time in the world. We didn't have to be afraid.

"Your hands are cold," he whispered. "Here." He let me slip them under his shirt to warm them. When he flinched I pulled them away, but he moved them back where they were.

"Shh. It's okay."

His chest was nothing like Alex's—it felt like real flesh, not granite. Once my hands warmed I smoothed them over his soft skin. "I've wanted to do this the first time you came over to my house."

"Mm," he murmured, "kiss me?" He traced his lips across my jaw. A thrill went through me, all the way to my feet.

"No," I answered honestly, "I just wanted to feel what your skin was like. I've only wanted to kiss you for the last few days."

"Why the last few days?" he asked, brushing his lips across my chin on the way back to my mouth, and I was so caught up in the smell and the touch and the feel of him, I answered without thinking.

"Louisa and you."

"Who?"

"Us. In a previous life."

And that did it.

David jerked back. "What?"

"Nothing. Never mind." I tried to slip my hands back under his shirt, but that wasn't happening anymore.

David held my hands at the wrists and shifted out from underneath me. "This whole thing is some sort of reincarnation fantasy?"

"No. David, this is reality. Forget what I said."

"Tell me what you meant." He leaned down to retrieve my crutches. He was serious.

I propped myself up again and took a breath. "Fine. It's nothing. It's just . . . clusters."

"Clusters," he repeated.

"People sometimes . . . travel in clusters. You know, life to life."

"According to my nutjob parents?"

"They're not nutjobs. The woman in the gray space said the same thing—I mean, she didn't call them clusters, but she said sometimes people . . . find each other again. And I think . . . that's us."

"The woman in the gray space?"

"The one I saw when I was dead."

David ran a hand through his hair. "I don't believe this—"

"I know you don't believe it," I said. "That's okay. It doesn't affect—" I motioned from him to me. "This. I want this separately. I mean, I want you for *you*—it doesn't matter about the past."

"You said you only wanted to kiss me because of—who was it?"

"Louisa and Henry," I said softly.

"Louisa and Henry. Right. Thanks. I'll be going now."

"Wait! David—" He had already started to walk away, but I grabbed his hoodie. "Look at me. Please."

He sighed and turned around.

"I like you, David. A lot. I think you're funny and smart and incredibly talented. I think you're brilliant, in fact. I'm sorry I didn't realize that when you first came here, but I realize it now."

"Because of some imaginary past-life regression."

"No, because of you. Because of your room. Because of your paintings. And because of tonight and how you kiss."

He shook his head and looked like he was starting to turn away again.

"Look," I said, "I know I've been a horrible bitch to you these past two years, and I'm really, really sorry about that. I'm mostly sorry for myself, because I could have had this a lot sooner."

"Cara, this whole thing is a mistake. I have to go."

"Why?"

He paused. I thought maybe he wouldn't have an answer for me, and that would mean I'd won—we could get back to how things were.

But he did have an answer.

"Because I don't want someone like you."

53

"You're doing it again," Beth told me this afternoon.

"What?"

"Your whole zombie routine."

"Oh. Sorry."

She's right. These past few days have been . . . unreal. I feel so spacey, like I'm not really rooted to the earth anymore. I've been more tired than I thought possible. More tired than after the most grueling of mogul events or triathlons or double headers. It's an exhaustion that reaches down to my soul. Which makes sense, because that's where it came from.

How am I supposed to deal with all of this?

In a way, I wish I didn't know. I wish I didn't know that Mrs. Mayer is carrying my daughter. Or that my daughter was the woman up there guiding me through the gray space. Or that I was in love with David.

Or that Alex was my killer.

Because it just doesn't seem possible to go about my business anymore, pretending I don't know who these people are. Every time I see Alex at school I wish the ceiling would cave in and crush him to death. I wish I really were on steroids so I could go over there and beat the living crap out of him. Before, I felt this mild disgust for him—okay, maybe a lot more than mild—but now it's like I dare him to come near me, because maybe there's a part of me that's on some vendetta against him, and I never knew it. Is that how it works? Do you carry a grudge from one lifetime to another, and worry about settling scores?

Is that what karma is? I thought karma always takes care of itself—you do something bad, you pay for it. But I suppose someone has to be the instrument of that punishment, right? The hand of God, down here on earth, slapping someone around.

"So," Beth said, laying out her usual bribe of dark and milk chocolate, "ready to talk about it?"

I sighed. "Yeah. But get ready—it's a long one."

I started with my last two sessions as Louisa.

"Wait," Beth said when I was finished with part one. "So your daughter in that life was the woman in the gray space, and now she's going to be the Mayers' daughter?"

"Yep."

"Whoa," Beth said.

We both needed another dose of chocolate.

Next I gave her the lowdown on David—David as Henry, not the current David. That was a whole other conversation.

"That's so romantic!" Beth said.

"Yeah, except for the part where Alex killed me because of it."

"Man, that guy is evil."

"Not much has changed," I said.

Beth gave me a strange look. "You don't think he'd still do something like that, do you? In this life?"

"You never know." But the real answer was yes, I do think that.

And finally it was time to talk about David. The current one.

She took it pretty well, considering her crush. But now that she knew David and I had a history together, it was easy for her to forfeit. And once I got to that certain point out at his car, all she seemed to care about was technique.

"How long did you kiss?" she wanted to know.

"I don't know, half an hour? Maybe longer—I sort of lost track."

"Wow . . ."

"Yeah, well, since that's the last time he'll ever kiss me, I'm glad we stretched it out."

"He'll kiss you again."

"Uh, no. You don't know David the way I do—he really despises all that woo-woo stuff. You didn't hear how he said it."

Beth nodded confidently. "He'll be back."

When I finally finished catching her up on everything, and all the chocolate was gone, Beth and I both lay back on my bed.

"Wow," Beth said, rubbing her stomach. "That's all really messed up."

"Tell me about it."

What's even more messed up is that I can't even go back to things as they were with David—back before the kiss, back to when we didn't talk much, but could at least hang out in the same area.

Now every time I come toward his table at lunch he simply gets up and leaves. So I end up sitting there alone, while I'm sure over at the jocks' table they're all dying of laughter to see the great Cara Campbell shunned by a loser.

But they don't know him.

And they can't possibly know how much it hurts.

I've tried to talk to him—at school, on the phone— but he's not interested. It's the total freeze-out. Hard to believe just a few nights ago I warmed my hands on his soft skin and finally found out what his lips taste like.

And it wasn't garlic.

This is unacceptable.

What does he think we're going to do for the next year and a half—ignore each other? Pretend none of this happened?

Plus there's the fact that I know something he doesn't: we have a bond. We've meant something to each other before, and we mean something to each other now. He can try to pretend otherwise, but the truth is the truth.

I need a ride.

54

Mrs. Mayer let me in.

"You look a lot better," I said.

"I've actually kept down two whole pieces of toast today."

"Yay, baby." *Yay, Baby Annie,* I could have said, but I think maybe that's going to stay my secret.

Mrs. Mayer smiled. "Which one of us are you here for?"

"David . . . eventually. But maybe you first?"

"Come on. Mark's writing. I just made tea."

I was sure she had no idea what had gone on between David and me, and I wasn't about to fill her in, but still, she had to guess there was some . . . connection. She knew as much about my past life as I did.

We settled down at the kitchen table, and Mrs. Mayer offered me cookies. "No, thanks. I just ate a pound of chocolate."

Baby Annie didn't really like the sound of that. Mrs. Mayer suddenly looked a little pale.

I hurried to get to the point, just in case our time was limited. "I need to ask you about . . . the whole David and me thing. I mean, what it's supposed to mean."

"David and you in the past," she said.

"Right."

Mrs. Mayer bobbed her tea bag. "Cara, don't take this the wrong way, but . . . I think it's easy to overread these things. Our research shows that the most we can say is that people who travel in clusters have important lessons to learn from each other."

"Oh." It was pretty much the same thing the woman in the gray space had told me. Only, at the time she and I were talking about it, I didn't realize I'd care so much. I didn't think to ask her any follow-up questions.

"Sometimes it means more," Mrs. Mayer conceded. "You saw some of the stories in the manuscript about couples who found each other after many years, but . . . I don't think we can generalize about that."

"Oh," I said again. It wasn't what I wanted to hear. I guess I was looking for some ammunition. "I thought maybe . . ." I felt embarrassed asking the guy's mother, but who else was going to know the answer? "So you don't think there's such a thing as soul mates?"

"I do," she said. "I'm just not sure we can say with certainty who those people are. I think it's up to us in each lifetime to decide who we belong with. And sometimes that can be more than one person over the course of the life. We might have different lessons we have to learn from different mates. You understand?"

"So is that why both Alex and David traveled with me? I still haven't learned what I need to from both of them?"

"Maybe," she said. "Or maybe they still need to learn from you."

It was a lot to absorb. We sat there in silence and sipped our tea for a while as I sorted through what she'd said, and how it compared to what I'd already come up with myself.

"So if we learn it—does that mean we won't see each other again next time?"

"I don't know," Mrs. Mayer admitted. "Maybe we still travel with the same people, but eventually have peace with them. Isn't that a nice thought?"

I'd rather not spend even a minute of another life with Alex, thank you. But I wouldn't mind seeing David again. Which I didn't say to his mother. I was already sounding pathetic enough with all my questions about him.

But I did have one more. "The other night . . . we were talking—David and I. And I sort of let slip about us knowing each other before."

Mrs. Mayer grimaced. "I can guess how that went."

"Right. He pretty much told me he didn't want to talk to me anymore."

"I'm sorry, Cara. Maybe I should have warned you—"

"No, I could have figured it out. I was just being . . . careless." Mostly because I'd just been making out with her son and my head was a bank of fog.

I drummed my fingers against the side of my cup. "So, now that I've ruined it . . . any advice?"

Mrs. Mayer smiled. "David is a wonderful young man."

"I agree."

"But very difficult at times."

Glad she's the one who said it. "I agree."

"I think you just have to be patient." She patted my hand. "But I think you'll find he's worth it."

What a weird conversation to be having. I've never in my life talked about a guy behind his back with his own mother.

"Why is he like that anyway?" I asked. "Why does he get so upset about past lives and near-death experiences and all of that? What difference does it make to him?"

"It's because of Jilly," Mrs. Mayer said. "I think he still . . . can't accept what happened."

"Then he should have been happy when that patient gave Dr. Mayer her message, right? You were."

"It's different for Davey," Mrs. Mayer said. "He still thinks he killed her."

55

"Davey was ten, Jilly was nine," Mrs. Mayer began. "With the two of them so close in age, they were always fighting and competing for something —who could watch their TV program that night, who got to have what they wanted for dinner, who got more birthday presents, who got to ride in front—

"And that was what the fight was about that day. They were carpooling with our neighbors the Wilsons that morning, and the whole fight during breakfast was about whose turn it was to sit up front. Jilly said Davey had had two turns in a row, Davey disputed that—it was all so ridiculous.

"Then when Margie Wilson drove up, Davey ran out of the house first and jumped into the front seat. Jilly started crying. I was going to be late for court and didn't have time to get involved. Jilly begged me to tell Davey to move to the back seat, but I told her they were old enough to work it out themselves.

"And then came the last thing she ever said to me," Mrs. Mayer mused. "Believe me, Cara, it's been stuck in my mind for seven long years. And it's why I believed Mark's patient immediately—she got every word of it right."

I was almost afraid to ask. "What did she say?"

"She screamed it at me, actually. 'You like Davey more than me! You always take his side! You're so unfair! I hate you!'" Mrs. Mayer smiled sadly. "You know how children keep score."

Actually, I don't know. I've never kept score with Beth. I wonder if she ever has with me.

"But it was an important lesson for me," Mrs. Mayer said. "About what I want my last moments with someone to be like. Trust me—Davey and Mark never get to leave this house without me telling them I love them."

"That's awful," I said. "I mean, not that you tell them you love them—"

"I know what you mean, honey. And yes, I agree." She gave my hand a squeeze. "But then the next thing Mark's patient said really gave me comfort. She said Jilly wanted me to know she was so sorry for what she said—she knew it wasn't true, and she didn't mean it."

"Wow."

"What amazes me—" Mrs. Mayer paused to clear her throat. She had been getting more emotional the longer we talked, but I could tell she was trying to fight it. "What amazes me is that my little girl found a way to tell me that. It took four years, but she found someone who was under her father's care, and she found a way to get through and tell us. Isn't that remarkable?"

I nodded. My whole body was one whole chill. That story was better than anything I'd read in their book.

"But why can't David be happy about it, too?" I asked. "You said before that Jilly told the patient to tell you she was happy—that everything was all right. Why didn't that make David happy?"

Mrs. Mayer smiled and shook her head. "You don't know Davey. He doesn't want to be off the hook. He believes he killed his little sister—if he'd let her sit in front, she'd still be alive—"

"And he'd be dead."

"Maybe. Or maybe he could have survived it—Davey has a whole scenario in his head."

"But . . . that's not how it works, is it? I mean, I died and I wasn't supposed to—I mean, medically. It was a freak thing. And I could have stayed dead, but I came back—because it wasn't my time yet. But it was Jilly's time, right? I mean, isn't that how it works?"

"I think so—now," Mrs. Mayer said. "But it took hearing from Jilly to recognize that. And then all the research we've been doing—the more I discover, the more I believe.

"But Davey . . . doesn't see it that way. He thinks we're chasing false hope. He thinks we're living in a fantasy just to avoid real life."

Yep. That was pretty much the impression I got from him, too. But I had no idea he had a personal stake in Jilly's death. I had no idea he felt so guilty.

"But why can't he—"

Mrs. Mayer abruptly stood up. "Sorry, I—" Without another word she fled the kitchen. It sounded like she barely made it to the bathroom in time.

I sat there alone, listening to the poor woman retch. And I figured I had three choices: call my mom to come pick me up; wait until Mrs. Mayer felt up to it, and ask her for a ride home—

Or climb the stairs.

56

The walls were blank.

"What did you do?" I shouted. "David! Are you crazy?"

He didn't even bother to turn around. He just kept measuring a section of blank wall and making pencil marks on it.

"David, what's going on?" I demanded. "Why did you do this? Where are your beautiful paintings?"

He ignored me and kept on measuring.

"David, answer me! Is this because of me?"

He turned around and fixed me with one of those unnerving gazes. "Not everything is about you, Cara. I do this all the time. I finish a painting, I paint over it, I start over. It's called learning."

His sarcasm made me want to punch him. "But . . . they were perfect! How could you do that?"

He had already returned to measuring and marking. "They were done," he said in a bored voice. "Time to move on."

It was all too much. I didn't care if I he wanted me there or not—I made my way to his bed and lay down. My head felt light. It wasn't enough that I just had to hear what Mrs. Mayer told me, but now to come up and see this. It was all too sad.

At least the stars were still there, above the bed. The room smelled of fresh paint—one of the walls was still wet with it. Plain white. How impossibly blank.

David just ignored me, which was fine. I wasn't there to fight. And I didn't even mind not talking, although that's what I'd come up to do. That bone-weariness had taken over again, and all I wanted to do was lie there and let the fumes make my headache even worse.

I must have slept, because when I opened my eyes again there was already a sketch up. It was of a massive horse—it took up the whole wall.

I propped myself up on my elbows. The sketch was some consolation—it was beautiful.

"Will you paint it?" I asked.

David flinched. I think maybe he forgot I was there.

"No, it's just a sketch," he said.

"Da Vinci?" I asked.

David nodded and kept working.

I stared at the figure forming under his hand. So smooth. So perfect. Not a line out of place.

"You're so . . ." I saw him pause, then catch himself and go back to drawing. "Brilliant. You're really incredible, David. I can't believe what you can do."

He pretended to ignore me while he shaded in one of the hooves.

"How long will that take?" I asked. The whole thing was mesmerizing to watch.

"A few days."

"And what will you do on the other walls?"

I think he was surprised we were having this conversation. Maybe he expected me to come up there and confront him about our "relationship." *It's coming, buddy. Wait for it.*

"Maybe *Virgin of the Rocks* here," he answered, pointing to the freshly-whitened wall. "And *Leda and the Swan* over there."

"All da Vinci?"

"Yeah."

"You really like his stuff, huh?"

"It's the best way to learn," David said.

"I can't wait to see them all."

But first there was the matter of him not wanting me around. David finally set down his pencil and gave me his full attention.

"Why are you here, Cara?"

I kept my voice light. "I needed to talk to your mother about something." Not really why I came there, but it did happen.

He didn't expect that.

"And now, I'm sorry to say, she's puking her guts out. So I was hoping just for the sake of kindness and the fact that we were actually kissing just a few nights ago—"

"Cara—"

Whatever it was, I wasn't going to let him say it. I needed to hang on to at least a little bit of my dignity. "I was hoping maybe you could give me a ride home. Just one last time."

He folded his arms and stared at me. And I pretended not to care. Lots of guys have looked at me in this lifetime. Why should this one make me so nervous?

"Please?" I added politely.

David sighed. "Fine."

I look forward to riding in the front seat of a car again one day. I almost said as much on the way to my house, just to make conversation, but that made me think of the story Mrs. Mayer had told me.

What must that be like, living with something like that? If I'd been fighting with Beth over where to sit, and she'd been plowed into and killed—how would I feel? Probably exactly like David did.

And that led me to the next thought: If I hadn't died

—if I hadn't had personal experience with the gray space and with the bodiless souls playing cards there—sorry, Life Poker—and then if I hadn't let Dr. Mayer hypnotize me, and gone back to that previous life—would I believe someone telling me Bethie had a message for me from beyond? Would I believe someone if they said she forgave me?

I guess it depended on whether there was some secret message, like the one Jilly had passed to Mrs. Mayer. If the last thing Beth had said to me was something specific like, "I hate you for never letting me sit in front. I hope you die a horrible death. And I want my blue sweater back," and then next thing you know, BAM, Bethie was killed—and then years later some mystic or psychic or someone repeated those exact words to me—wouldn't I believe? I would, wouldn't I?

So what was David's problem? Why couldn't he at least *consider* the idea that maybe his sister didn't blame him?

And since David certainly wasn't talking to me on the way home, I had time to let my mind drift to the rest of my conversation with Mrs. Mayer—about why it is David and Alex and I are together again in this lifetime. It's not because Alex and I are soul mates—I can guarantee that. But the idea that maybe we still have to learn something from each other—yeah, I guess I buy that.

And David? Soul mate or not? I loved him in one life

—does that mean I'm supposed to love him in this one? Is he supposed to love me? And if not, what's left? What are we supposed to learn from each other?

I was poking along in my brain with that thought, bumping it from one side of my skull to the other, when finally I got it.

I mean, I *got it*.

I'm so stupid. So self-centered. So incredibly dense sometimes.

Why did I see David's face when I woke up? Why is David in my life? What am I supposed to learn from David?

It's not me. I'm not the one who's supposed to learn.

It's him. I'm here to teach him.

I waited until we were in front of my house.

"David, turn off the car."

57

"You remember how a few weeks ago you called me a clone?"

"Cara, I'm not interested in fighting with you."

"This isn't a fight. I just want to know—do you still think that about me?"

He sighed. "No."

"Okay. Thank you. But do me a favor: how would you describe the kind of person I was until recently?"

"There's really no point—"

"David, two nights ago you had your tongue down my throat. I think you can spare me a few minutes of conversation, don't you think?"

Big sigh this time. "Fine."

"So how would you have described me? Go ahead—it's not going to hurt my feelings." *Much.*

He listed them off as if he were already bored with the whole topic. "Shallow, self-absorbed, conceited, self-aggrandizing, elitist—"

"Okay, that's enough," I interrupted before he could really get going. "Would you have called me . . . spiritual?"

"No."

"Or interested in weird things like psychic phenomena or reincarnation?"

"I don't really know what you were into, Cara. Other than yourself."

Nice to know what people really think of you. But I did ask.

"Well, just believe me when I say I never thought about any of that stuff—the afterlife, any of it. I didn't believe in any of that."

"If that's what this is going to be about, you might as well leave right now."

I punched the back of his seat. "Would you just listen for once? I don't understand you, David. One minute you're out here kissing me like you can't get enough of me, and the next you're freaking out just because I accidentally said something about reincarnation."

"I didn't freak out—"

"Look, all I'm saying is I'm sorry you don't agree with what your parents think, but I've had my own experiences now, and I'm just trying to figure it all out."

"Great," David said. "No one's stopping you. Have a good time. Now would you get out?"

"God, you are so frustrating!" This wasn't going at all like I wanted it to. Forget trying to be delicate—I just went for it.

"Look, I know all about Jilly. I know how she died, I know you think it was your fault—"

David whipped around in his seat. "Shut up! It's none of your business."

"It is my business. Because I realize now the real reason I was supposed to become friends with you was for you, not me. You needed to hear what I had to say."

David opened his door. He came around to my side and opened mine. "Get out. This isn't funny."

I laughed. "You think I'm trying to be funny? I'm trying to help you, David."

"I don't need your help."

He reached in and was ready to haul me out when suddenly a car rounded the corner and shone its headlights right on us.

"Shit." I recognized the car, of course. I just didn't realize he was still driving past my house at night. I wondered if he'd seen David and me kissing. But no, he wouldn't have just hidden and watched—he would have done exactly what he was doing now.

Alex screeched to a halt beside David's car. The stereo blasted. Alex's buddy Dan sat beside him. They both held open cans of Bud.

"What're you doing, Mayer?"

"Throwing your girlfriend out of my car. You?"

Alex didn't like that. Neither did I.

I slapped David's hand away and craned my head back to look at Alex. "Get out of here. I've already told you to leave me alone."

"You f—ing him?" Alex demanded.

"I'm not f—ing anyone," I said, "and it's none of your business what I do anymore. We're DONE, Alex. How many thousand times do I have to tell you that?"

"Then what's he doing here?" Alex demanded.

"What are *you* doing here?" I shot back. "Aren't the quarter-finals tomorrow? I thought you had curfew."

Alex ignored me. He was too busy glaring at David. "Keep your hands off her, faggot."

David laughed. I wanted to tell him that wasn't a good idea.

Alex leaned further across Dan. He jabbed his finger toward David. "I said you'd better f—ing keep away from her, asshole."

David turned to me. "This is boring. Please get out now. I'm going home."

I scooted down the seat toward the door. David handed me my crutches. Alex was eerily quiet.

When I was out and upright I looked over at his car. Alex was draining the last of his Bud.

He crooked his finger at me, motioning me to come over. I decided to try David's method and just laugh.

Even though my heart was pounding. It's generally not good to disobey Alex—especially not when he's been drinking.

"Dammit, Cara, get over here!" At least he hadn't called me babe.

I stood my ground. And was surprised to find David's leg suddenly pressing into mine.

As if I needed the encouragement. There was no way I was going near Alex.

I flashed on those last few minutes—Louisa's fear and pain, and little Annie's screams. No, I was staying where I was.

"Go home," I told Alex in as bored a tone as I could muster. "You're drunk. You need to be fresh for tomorrow."

Alex brightened at that, the idiot. "You coming to watch?"

"No."

He scowled. "F—ing bitch." He revved his motor, and that's how I knew it was almost over. I leaned a little more into David's leg.

Alex pointed at David one more time. "I'll f—ing kick your ass."

David just kept his hands in his pockets and didn't respond.

Alex glared at me one more time, then flipped us both off before ripping out of there.

I sagged against David. He caught me with an arm

around my waist.

"I need to sit down."

"I'll take you inside," David said.

"No, I'm not leaving until you listen to me."

5 8

I died, I told him. For forty-two seconds. I told him the whole story.

And maybe thanks to Alex, David was too tired to fight me too much. He just sat there in the front seat and gazed out the windshield at the dark while I lay in back and recited my story to the ripped up car ceiling.

"Are you through?" he said quietly when I finally got to the part about waking up and seeing his face.

I wished I were through. I felt worn to the bone. I could have happily gone inside and collapsed onto my bed and slept until noon. But I knew I might never have this chance with David again. So I told him, "Almost."

And then I gave him the story of David and Louisa. And Alex. And baby Annie. But I didn't tell him the last part—the part about where she is right now. I know everyone has their limits, and I had probably already exceeded David's.

I ended with me dead again. And up in the gray space to wait until I was ready for another life—which might have been all the way to this one, considering everything that had happened to Louisa.

It was a few minutes before David said anything. "Are you done now?"

"I suppose so."

"Why do you think I would care about any of this?" David asked.

I guess I shouldn't have been surprised by his rudeness anymore. It's just that I hoped somehow our little makeout session the other night had at least softened him toward me. Apparently not.

"I'm telling you all this," I said, "because I don't think you understand about death. You seem to think you had some control over what happened to Jilly—"

"Don't talk to me about my sister," David snapped, finally whipping around to look at me. "You don't know anything about it."

"I know you didn't kill her. She was going to die anyway—"

"Don't give me any of that 'It was her time' bullshit. 'It was God's will'—you know how many times I had to hear that? I know what happened."

"So do I. I've been dead, David. I'm not making it up, that's real—you can check the hospital records. So I am uniquely in a position to tell you that I know what death is like, and I know with absolute certainty there was nothing you could have done differently that day to save her. You're not the reason she died. You could have hidden her in a closet or shipped her to the moon, and it was still going to happen."

"Why?" he demanded.

"Because that's how it works. You think I couldn't have died a hundred different times in my life? I've been climbing on dangerous cliffs, I've skied where there are avalanches, I've kayaked over waterfalls—it could have happened any day. And when I died on the operating table, I could have stayed dead. It wasn't up to me."

"Then why bother trying to save anyone?" David sneered. "Why don't we just let everyone die?"

"Because sometimes saving a person is the way it's supposed to go that day. Like the doctors shocking me back to life."

David groaned. "See, this is the kind of bullshit argument I hate. When someone dies, it's preordained. When they live, it's preordained. There's no order to it."

I laughed. "You think this is a math problem? Of course there's no order to it."

The whole thing was exhausting. Plus, I had been lying there in a freezing car for nearly an hour, barely moving, and my whole body was stiff and cold. Next time I plan on holing up in a guy's car for a long philosophical argument I need to remember a blanket.

I decided to get back to the real reason I was telling him all of that.

"Look, David, whether you believe it or not, I actually care about you. I probably shouldn't anymore, considering what a complete jerk you were to me the other night, but whatever." I pressed on before he could answer that. "The point is, I am the only person you know who can tell you what it's like to be dead. And I can tell you with a hundred percent certainty that your little sister didn't blame you. She isn't up there wishing you a horrible life, or cursing your name, or holding some grudge. The second she died it was over. She was peaceful. I've been there—I know."

David's jaw tightened. I couldn't tell if he was angry or just sick of hearing me say things he didn't want to hear.

"Think of it this way," I said, hoping maybe someone else's reasoning would sound better than mine. "It's like standing on the shore and staring out at the ocean. You see a lot of it, but you still can't ever see it all. It's like that with Jilly's death—you think you know everything that happened that day, but you don't. You can't. I'm the best proof you have that there are things out there that you have no idea about. And maybe instead of dismissing them you should actually try to figure them out."

He didn't say anything. I guess I didn't really expect him to.

But I was freezing, and couldn't wait any longer.

"I have to go now," I told him. "Could you please help me with the door?"

David came around to my side and helped me out. Unlike right before Alex showed up, this time he was gentle about it. I leaned against the car while he handed me my crutches. It reminded me all too well of the last time we'd been in this position.

"Thanks for listening," I said. "I appreciate that."

It was too dark to see his face clearly. But I could feel his breath. It was warm and close to my cheek, and it reminded me of the other night, too.

David crossed his arms over his chest and leaned back beside me. Just like before.

My body shivered.

"You should go inside," he said quietly.

"Yeah. Okay."

I waited one more moment, just in case. But he didn't move.

"Okay, good night." My voice sounded hoarser than I meant it to. I made my way slowly toward my house, and he didn't try to stop me.

Damn.

59

He hasn't called. I guess I didn't really expect him to. I mean, if you look at it, I've always been the one chasing him—calling him, going over to his house, kissing him. That's a first for me.

Probably a last, too, considering how it's turned out.

But at least I said what I wanted to say. If he chose not to hear it, I can't really do anything about that.

So it's Sunday, and Pinedale won the quarter-finals last night, of course. Which means the town is pretty much shut down today for the barbecues, the bonfires, the beer fests, the drunken vandalism, the drunken everything. Fun, fun, fun as long as no one actually sets themselves on fire. It'll get even worse over the next two weekends if they win the semis and then the finals. But at least there'll be a parade.

I had to break it to my parents that we're disinvited from all the Toomys' parties. They weren't too happy about that. My mom said she hopes I'll work things out with Toomy as soon as possible, since "you girls have been so close all your lives. I'd hate to see you lose out on such a wonderful friendship." By which I assume she means she'd like to make sure we're at least invited to their Christmas party next month.

But maybe I'm just in a bad mood.

Part of it is I've been slacking off again. I feel all soft and squishy. I've only missed a couple of days of weight training, but every day matters. So when Beth and my parents take off for the barbecue next door tonight—pizza and a keg, instead of the Toomys' fancy catered affair, but oh, well—I'm going to give myself an extra hard workout. Time to get back to focusing on the machine.

We get the bodies we need in this lifetime, Mrs. Mayer said. To learn what we need to learn.

I've been thinking about that.

Ever since I came back from the dead, I've thought I was wrong to want to be an Athlete. I thought there must be something better for me out there—something more noble. But then I look at David, and I see someone who could have picked either Mathematician or Artist—and who's to say one is better than the other? Isn't David allowed to choose which one he's the most passionate about? If that's the test, then my answer is easy.

I could be a lot of things. I have the brains and the grades to go a lot of different ways— Doctor, Lawyer, Engineer, Teacher—the list is probably long.

But what does my soul really want?

It picked this body for a reason. It picked a girl who would grow to be five-foot-nine, who would have strong bones and muscles, who would have the coordination and balance to master any number of physical tests.

And it picked a personality with drive. I am not a Type-A Anal Overachiever by accident. I have a personality that not only accepts a challenge, but actually craves it. I know not everybody is like that. Beth isn't—she's brilliant as a musician, and she loves what she does, but she doesn't try to make it harder for herself by playing upside down blindfolded in a wind tunnel.

And see, I would. I like it when it's hard—in fact, I prefer it when it's impossible. I like to push myself harder and longer than anyone else, and see what I can do.

Those same traits might make me an excellent Doctor or Lawyer or Engineer, etc., but I don't want that. I want to move. I want to climb and run and jump and ski and swim and fly. That is who I am, down to the smallest particles of the blob of light of my soul.

And if I forgot to bring that one missing ingredient—the ace of hearts, my courage—the first time I came down to this life, then I'm glad I was able to go back for it, and now I'm ready to go on.

What was my wrong turn? What did the woman mean by that?

It wasn't in deciding to be who I am—I get that now. I haven't really had a choice. As sure as I'm sure of anything, I picked the Athlete card and that's the life I will play out as long as I'm here on earth.

I think my wrong turn was letting myself be afraid. That's why I had to die and come back.

I'm not afraid anymore. I know this life will play out as it will. I'm not afraid of dying, and I can't be afraid of living. Maybe my life won't always be easy or happy. Maybe I'll always be alone. Maybe I won't have friends anymore. Maybe the only person who will ever truly love me is Beth. Maybe David and I could have been together in this lifetime if I'd handled it differently, but I didn't, so oh well. And maybe Mrs. Mayer is right anyway, and the only reason David and I keep running into each other is to learn some new lesson from each other. And now I guess we're done.

So that's just how it is. Life goes on.

And it's time I go live it how I want to.

60

There are no coincidences.

It's not a coincidence that Pinedale won last night. It's not a coincidence that Alex and his buddies celebrated in typical style by getting completely smashed. It's not a coincidence that Alex saw me with David on Friday night and came to the wrong conclusion.

It isn't a coincidence that I did a one-hour brutal session on my arms tonight, and another hour on my legs. Or that I decided to go without my brace for the rest of the night, and see how it felt in the morning.

And although I might tell people differently, it's not a coincidence that when I heard the pebbles against my window, I didn't even hesitate about going down.

Something in me.

He was still drunk, of course.

"What are you doing here?" I asked.

"You weren't at the party."

"No, I wasn't."

He slumped against the side of the door. "I miss you. You're driving me crazy."

"We broke up, Alex, remember?"

"That's bullshit. You f—ing Mayer now?"

"No," I said.

"Damn right. You're mine."

And then because the topic of our relationship wasn't interesting enough to him, he launched into a drunkard's highlight reel of all the glories of the game I missed. "You shoulda seen me—I was great!"

I just stood there and listened. There was nothing to be afraid of.

"Are you done?" I asked calmly.

He made a pouty face. "Doncha wanna hear?"

"No. Goodnight."

I started to close the door. He batted it open. "C'mon, babe! Come outside with me. I wanna celebrate."

And there it was. I had the choice. I could have said no. Could have called for my parents if Alex had made a scene. Could have done a lot of things, but what I did was put on my coat.

There was frost on the ground. The rubber tips of my crutches crunched across our lawn.

Alex bundled his arms around himself and pretended to shiver. "Cold."

I didn't say anything. It was like I was watching from above. Like I was up there in the gray space and had just cleared away a section with my sleeve. It was like watching war. No sound, just the grisly ballet of bodies losing their souls.

We have a spot. It's around the side of my house, in one of those free-standing utility sheds people buy to keep their extra stuff clean but out of the way. Ours is for my all my sporting gear. Alex and I have spent many a night in there, working out amidst the smell of my sweat.

It's hard to say who was leading whom. I have no doubt I wanted to go. Alex was practically giddy, thinking I had forgotten and forgiven everything.

My leg ached from the cold and from not being in its brace. But I wasn't going to break the spell. We were heading toward a moment that I couldn't clearly see, but I knew that moment would come.

I felt above the door frame for the key and unlocked the padlock. There are florescent lights in there, but I didn't turn them on.

Alex went straight into the routine. He pulled down a quilted blanket where I kept it stored on a top shelf, and laid it on the concrete floor.

"Careful of my leg," I said almost absent-mindedly. I pointed to it so he would remember which one.

Alex helped me down onto the floor.

His fingers were too drunk to handle the buttons on my coat. I had to help him.

He whispered things in my ear. Things I didn't use to mind. Or maybe I did. I can't remember.

He fumbled with his pants. I could see his teeth grinning in the dark.

"You hurt me," I said.

"Huh?" He kept fumbling.

"I told you I didn't want to, and you forced me."

"What're you talking about?"

"My leg."

"I told you you shouldna run."

"Let's talk," I said, and I pushed him off more gently than I wanted to.

Alex grunted. "C'mon. Later."

"No, now." I pushed him harder.

Alex pushed back.

My arms were still pumped from their workout. I wasn't afraid. I shoved Alex off me.

"F—ing bitch!" He rolled back on top of me, just like I knew he would.

He pinned my good leg with his knee. He held my arms over my head with one hand and with the other pulled up my shirt.

There are no coincidences. I was born to like things difficult.

My body is a thing of beauty. It has always done what I asked of it. Even when I think I'm too tired or too hurt to go on, if I ask it to, it will persevere.

Day after day my injured leg has only bent in small degrees. I didn't want to push it. I've been grateful for what it could give me.

But now I needed much more.

"You ruined my leg," I told Alex. He was busy hurting me in other ways. He's too stupid to do more than one thing at a time. There are no coincidences.

The yellow light burned bright in my chest. My body would recover. I was going to be an Athlete in this life, no matter what happened in the next few seconds, so I had nothing to lose. And a whole lifetime to gain.

My brain told it to move, and move hard and fast. My leg bent where it hadn't, drove upward when it couldn't, brought with it all the force and strength in my body and all the strength and will of my soul.

It drove up so hard Alex froze for a moment. I could see his eyes widen in the dark. Time is a line, stretching out forever, and while he hesitated in Time, I did not.

My life is endless. This body may wear out, but I will not. My soul is quick and sturdy, and even though my body might not have been ready to move yet, it did because I told it to.

We—my soul, my body, and I—flung Alex off us and

bolted for the door and ran out into the cold. We were barely clothed, and that was fine. We ran on a damaged leg, but the pain was silent, like watching a silent war. We ran into the house and we shouted, and the lights came on and the parents came down.

It felt like a movie. My father in this lifetime chased my former husband across the lawn. Even an out-of-shape car salesman can sometimes take down a drunk football player. My mother in this lifetime called the police. And the daughter—that's me—told them every-thing. Because finally it all made sense.

My mission in this lifetime is to tell the truth. To go back to where I took a wrong turn and have the courage to make it right. The wrong turn wasn't Alex—I think we were destined to meet again, just like I was destined to meet David for whatever reason. I don't even think the wrong turn was letting Alex hurt me again—I didn't know he was going to do it, and maybe it's like I told David about Jilly—it was going to happen no matter what. Because it had to—I had to fix it this time so I won't keep replaying this part of my life over and over again.

Because I lied. I said Alex and I were just playing around, racing each other to prove I was still faster. I said it was an accident—I fell wrong, he tripped over me, it was my fault. I told them Alex felt horrible—how he stayed with me until the ambulance came, and finally I made him go home.

All lies. Because I was afraid of what Alex would do to me.

But I wasn't afraid anymore.

And suddenly I realized I was wrong about what I'd said to the woman in the gray space. I thought I was supposed to change the world by telling the truth. But really I was just supposed to change *my* world.

So I told them—my parents, Beth, the police: How he chased me. How he tackled me. How he pinned me down and forced me. How my leg bent under me, a sickening angle, the snap, the tear. How he ran off when he realized how injured I was. Because he was afraid I was going to tell. How he tried to pretend afterward it had never happened that way. How I let him pretend.

Time stretched out forever. I answered all their questions. But it still wasn't the whole truth.

Because now I finally understand what the whole truth is.

The woman in the gray space—my daughter—she waited for me. To warn me.

She could have gone on, just like everyone else playing the game, but she waited because she knew me. And she knew I was with Alex again, and wanted to help me get away. Forever this time, so I'd never have to go through it again.

Maybe that's what we do for each other. Maybe we come back and save each other, one person at a time.

This time it was her turn to save me. Maybe next time I'll save her.

And maybe this time I'm supposed to save David somehow. I thought I tried, but maybe not hard enough.

Maybe I'm supposed to keep trying until it works. Maybe that's why I was born liking things to be impossible.

61

"Hey," Beth whispered. "You awake?"

"No," I moaned. It took a minute, but eventually I gave in and opened my eyes. My room was dark. "What time is it?"

"A little after seven."

"At night?"

"Yeah." Beth handed me a cup of hot chocolate. "You've been sleeping a long time, and . . . I thought you might want to get up for a while."

The pain pills had knocked me out. Last time I looked, my knee was the size of Brazil. At least the doctor said I hadn't reinjured it too badly. I'll just have to wear the brace a lot longer.

I took a few sips of hot chocolate. I tasted a little

coffee in there, too—perfect. My head was one big whooze. My teeth felt like they were covered in grass.

"He's here," Beth said.

A chill raced through me. For a second I thought she meant Alex. But that was impossible. Alex had been arrested.

"Who?"

"David. He's been here since after school. Poor guy —he had to listen to me practice that Tchaikovsky piece about a hundred times."

"He's in your room?" My head was starting to clear.

"Not now. He's downstairs. But Mom's about to serve dinner, and . . . it's getting kind of weird."

"Help me change."

I hoped I didn't smell too bad. My mother stayed home from work today, and one of our tasks before I passed out was to wrap my leg, brace and all, in a couple of garbage bags and duct tape so I could finally take a long hot shower. I wanted to wash the whole night away. Erase the last of Alex's fingerprints.

Beth helped me into the bathroom so I could brush my teeth and splash the sleep off my face. I swiped on some deodorant, threw my hair into a ponytail, and that was good enough. I didn't have to be perfect. Then she helped me into my old rugby skirt, some wool socks, and a sweatshirt. Glamour girl. Glamour girl post-night from hell.

"Okay," I said, "bring him up."

His uniform had changed a little. Same jeans, same black Converses, same white t-shirt, but now a gray wool V-neck sweater instead of the hoodie. His hair was its usual windblown mess. He looked good. Really good.

"Hi."

"Hi." He'd never been in my room before. He looked uncomfortable.

I'd thrown my bedspread over the sheets so I could sit on top without looking like such an invalid. Beth had fluffed all my pillows into a pile behind me to prop me up. Now she stood in the doorway waiting for David to commit. As soon as he took a step inside, she flashed me a conspiratorial smile and softly shut the door behind him.

He stayed where he was.

"Um, want to sit down?" I pointed to the space at the bottom of my bed.

"Won't it . . . hurt?" he asked, eyeing my pumpkin-sized knee.

"No. Just be careful."

He was. He kept one foot on the floor and barely made a dent in my mattress.

"David, seriously—it's okay. I've got enough pain pills in me to last through the summer." Which was unusual for me. I usually don't take them—I prefer having a clear head—but somehow for this injury I didn't mind being out of it.

I gave David a couple of moments to see if he wanted to jump in there with some conversation, but that's never been his style. So I just kept going.

"I suppose it's all over school."

"Oh, yeah," he said.

"And everyone hates me?"

"Pretty much."

"Do they think I'm lying?" I asked, not really wanting to hear the answer.

David shrugged. "I'm not exactly linked into the high school gossip network. Although the consensus seems to be you could have waited until after the football championship."

Figures.

"Do you?" I asked, my mouth suddenly dry in a way I couldn't blame on the pills. "Think I'm lying?"

David finally leveled his eyes on me. "Of course not."

Which was the nicest thing he's ever said to me.

I relaxed a little, and so did he. He kicked off his shoes without asking me if that was cool (it was), and went ahead and took up more room on my bed. He bounced it a little too much for my leg's liking, but I wasn't going to show it. I didn't want to scare him off.

I wasn't entirely sure why he was there. Pity? Curiosity? He didn't seem the pitying or the gawking kind.

But whatever it was, he didn't seem in a hurry to tell

me. I've never met someone so comfortable with silence.

"How's your mom?" I asked, just to get him talking.

"Fine. She—actually, both of them—wanted to know that you were all right."

Oh. So that was it—he was on a mission of mercy from his parents. Well, that was nice of them.

I slouched back against my pillows. No point in worrying about how I looked anymore.

"Would you throw me that blanket?" I asked. "My feet are cold." Might as well get a favor out of him before he left.

David got up and retrieved the blanket from my chair. And then what he did next surprised me. He not only draped it over my legs, but he brought the rest of it up and tucked it around me, like he actually cared whether I got cold. That felt nice.

I gave him what I'm sure was a puzzled look. "Thanks."

He lingered there a moment longer, his hands on the back of my shoulders where he'd tucked the blanket, and he shifted his eyes to mine again. "Cara, I'm really sorry."

A charge went through me. I looked into his eyes and tried to read what was there.

"It's okay," I answered, taking a guess. "It doesn't hurt that much."

"That's not what I'm talking about," David said, his eyes softening at the edges, "and you know it."

I took a breath. "Okay."

"I don't like talking about my sister."

"I got that," I said.

"But I appreciate what you tried to do," he said.

"Okay."

David returned to the base of my bed. He settled in gently, then slipped his hands beneath the blanket. He folded his hands over my sock-covered toes. "Warm yet?"

I shook my head, even though suddenly my whole body felt warm.

He rubbed my feet, being very careful not to jiggle my bad leg. That plus the pain pills made it very hard to concentrate.

"I've thought a lot about what you said the other night," David continued.

My voice felt thin. "Which part?"

"The part about how you're the only person I've ever known who actually died and can tell me about it. That's a decent argument."

"Thank you." I cleared my throat and shifted my feet. "Okay, they're fine now." If we were going to have a serious discussion, I needed my head back. That wasn't going to happen while he was touching such a sensitive body part.

He tucked the blanket around my feet again, then

left his hand on top of my good shin. That wasn't much better.

"Do you know anything about da Vinci?" David asked. That snapped my brain back around.

"Um, what?"

"He wasn't just an artist. He was the original Renaissance Man—painter, musician, engineer, inventor, scientist, mathematician—"

"Sounds familiar."

"I've always really admired him," David said. "And tried to . . . live up to his example. You know?"

I nodded. I had no idea where this was going. And David's hand was still warm on top of my leg.

"One of the things he did," David continued, "was study anatomy. He wanted to make sure he painted the body as precisely as possible, and the only way to do that was to understand as much about it as he could. So he was always watching people—how they moved, what their faces looked like—but he also studied corpses. He wanted to see what was inside—how the muscles worked, what the bones and organs looked like."

I decided to try David's style of conversation, and just sit there and listen. That seemed to suit him fine. And he was back to absent-mindedly massaging my foot through the blanket. It felt good. I let him.

"But one of the autopsies he performed—he had to wait a little while."

"What do you mean?"

"The guy was still alive."

"Eww."

David smiled. "No, not 'eww.' Leonardo did that on purpose. He wanted to see what death was like. So he went to a hospital and stayed by the bedside of an old guy as he was dying. The man died very peacefully. Leonardo wanted to understand why that was.

"So he cut him open right away," David said. "He wanted to understand the mechanics of death—what happened to the heart, the brain, all of that. But he also wanted to look for the soul."

Now the chill that went through me had nothing to do with David touching me. I sat up a little straighter. "Your hero believed in the soul."

David looked at me shyly. "Yeah."

The competitor in me couldn't help it: I smelled victory.

"And all this time you've been acting like we're all crazy."

"Hold on," David said. "I didn't say he found it."

"But he believed enough to look for it."

"Yeah," David said. "And that was what I realized the other night after everything you said. Da Vinci kept these notebooks, filled with thousands of entries— questions he wanted answers to, like how birds fly, why thunder lasts longer than lightning, how he could build something so he could breathe underwater—anything and everything that occurred to him that he wanted answers to.

"But one of his main principles in all of that," David said, "was that he always forced himself to think about everything from scratch. He never wanted to make assumptions. So even when he thought he already knew the answer to something, he still investigated to make sure he was right. He never wanted to believe in a lie."

David locked eyes with me in that direct and unnerving way he has. It almost distracted me from what he said next.

"He even observed himself as he was dying—so he could make sure he understood what death really felt like."

That's when I got it. "And here I am."

"And here you are." David softly smiled.

"Your own personal experiment."

"Yep."

I gazed into those deep brown eyes of his and couldn't help thinking of Louisa. No, not Louisa, but me, watching her life. When David had walked into her house, I had no doubt it was him. I could see through his blue eyes all the way into that naked blob of light he really is. And now in this life he's dressed in warm, milk-soft skin, brown hair and brown eyes, Artist and Mathematician, a mouth that knows how to kiss me, a brain that knows how to challenge me, parents I needed to meet, and a little sister who's coming and I already know. David thinks there's no order to life? It looks as simple as math to me.

I told myself I wasn't going to chase him anymore, and I didn't have to. I stayed where I was, tucked up under my blanket, and he carefully crawled up the bed toward me. Then he leaned over and began by saying, "I'm sorry."

"So you believe me?" I asked, as the first of his kisses brushed my cheek. I didn't really want to talk anymore, but I had to make sure where we stood.

"I believe you believe," he answered, his fingers moving to the nape of my neck.

I caught his wrist and made him stop. "That's not good enough."

He kissed my temple, then my cheekbone, and then whispered in my ear, "I'm going to start from scratch. Keep an open mind. Teach me everything you know."

Time is a line stretching out. And it bends and it loops and comes back. And maybe I've known David twice now, or maybe a hundred times more. It doesn't matter how far we go back. All I care about is how far we go forward.

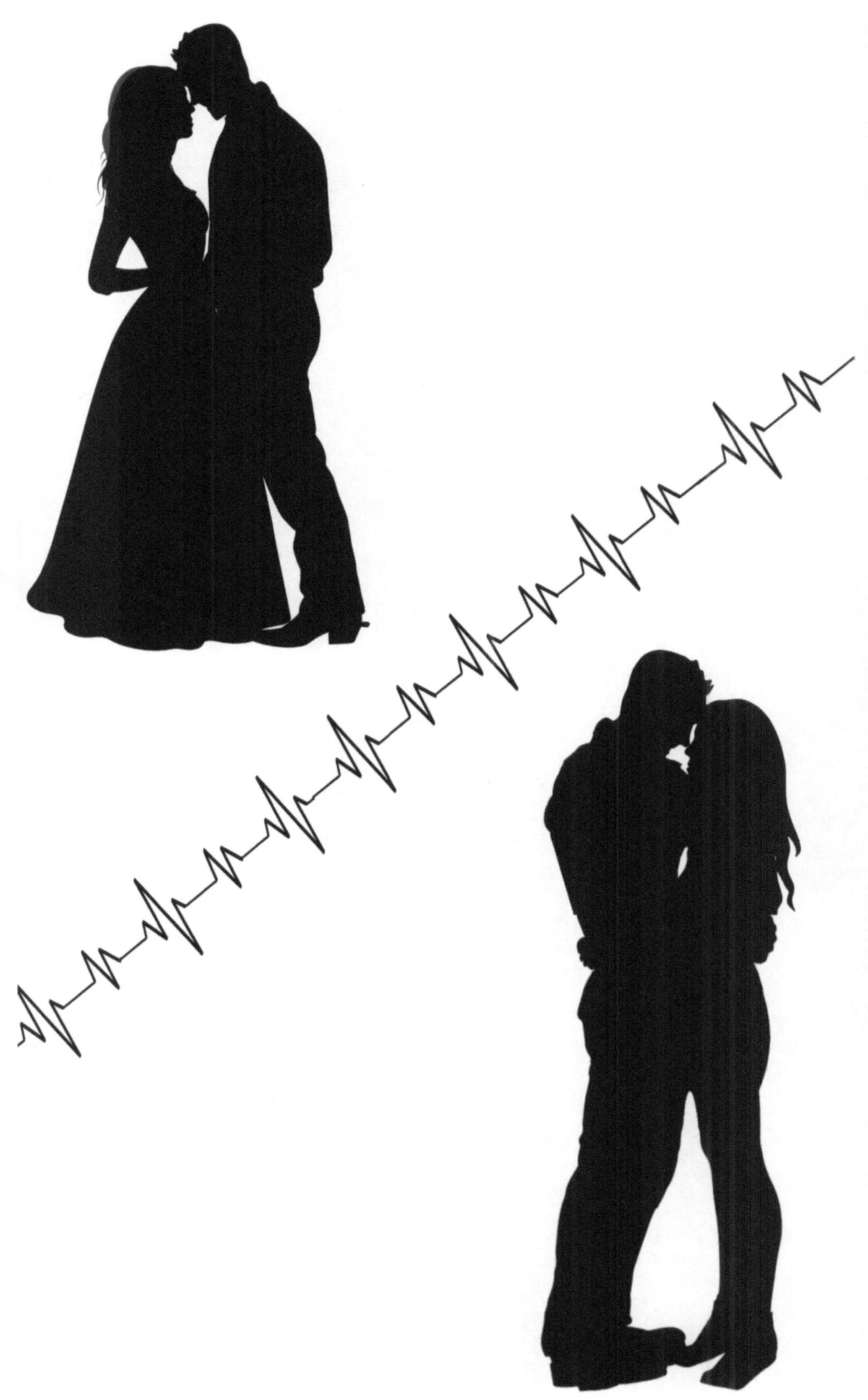

In a parallel universe...

What if you could meet a parallel version of yourself?

Mena's first week of high school?

DISASTER

But things are about to evolve...

An experiment so bold, anyone might think it was a little CRAZY...

Riley is an expert with dogs.
With people? Not at all.
But maybe her dogs can help her
finally find her own pack.

Embrace your nerd

Sleep-Read-Repeat

About the Author

Award-winning author Robin Brande is a former trial attorney, martial artist, Reiki Master, and wilderness medic. She writes in multiple genres, including young adult, mystery, fantasy, and science fiction.

She is also a designer and maker whose work celebrates the bookish life.

You will find all of her many books and designs at:
RobinBrande.com